C. L. EASTON

STRANGERS OF THE CROWD

STRANGERS OF EASTWOOD BOOK THREE

Strangers of the Crowd

Copyright © 2023 by C L Easton

Cover Design: Black Pirate Book Cover

Publisher: Black Rose Publishing

Ebook ISBN: 978-1-998910-02-1

Paperback ISBN: 978-1-998910-03-8

NOTE FROM THE AUTHOR

This book is written in Canadian English

This is the conclusion from the second book.
Strangers of the Town.

Take warning this is a dark romance. Please
read Books one and two before this one.

It includes:
Drug and Alcohol use, Public Sex, Rope
Bondage, Anal play, Graphic Sex, Orgasm
Denial, Group Sex, Graphic Murder, Torturing,
Gore, Blood, Flashbacks to childhood abuse.

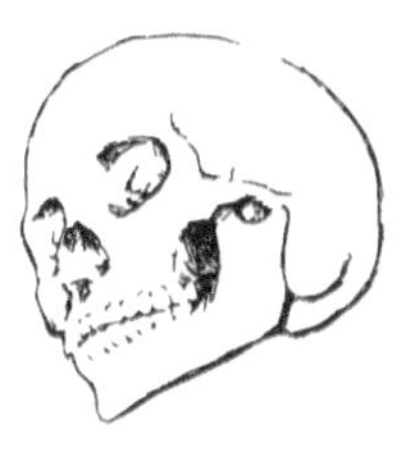

Having a shitty day? Remember you're somebody's reason to masturbate.

PLAYLIST

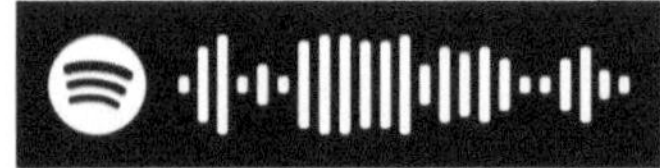

Me and the Devil- Soap&Skin
Burning Desire- Lana Del Rey
Gooey- Glass Animals
Nightmare- Avenged Sevenfold
JEKYLL & HIDE- Bishop Briggs
Heaven Without You- KID BRUNSWICK
Free Animal- Foreign Air
Dead Inside- Younger Hunger
beetlejuicebeetlejuicebeetlejuice- Life After Life
Bruises- Lewis Capaldi
Lonely Day- System of A Down
Train- Brick + Mortar
Sarcoma Killstation
Maybe, I- Des Rocs
Miss Murder- AFI

Scan the BarCode for More

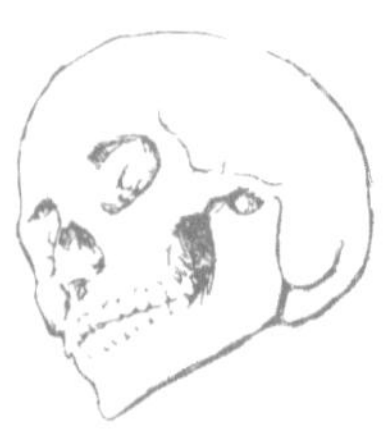

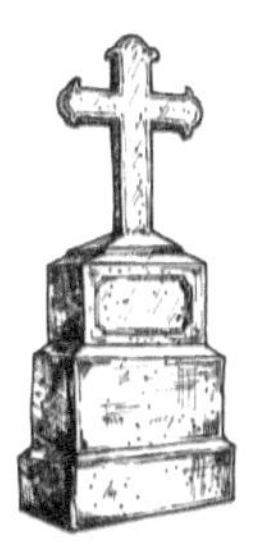

Prologue

COLE

"Will you shut the fuck up already?" I whispered.

I swear to God, working with your friends is complete torture.

"Sorry man, it's not my fault. It's cramped in here, and I'm a giant compared to you," Dorian hissed.

When I told Henry to figure his shit out with the gang and us, he did. It's now an MC with Conrad on board. It was an easy transition, although some were hesitant to want to switch. Most were excited. The town is a lot more welcoming to an MC than a gang. Dorian and I are still enforcers, Nyx wanted to quit and stay in school full time, but Catalina convinced him to stay in the club and school.

Instead of having him here tonight, it's Dorian complaining. I rub my forehead, getting frustrated. All we had to do was some recon. Another drug house has moved in, or so we suspect they have. We aren't sure, so we are sitting in Catalina's Volkswagen. We needed a car that sorta blends in. We've been here for three hours, and not a single person has come to the door looking to buy.

"I don't think there is a drug house. If it is, then they do deals somewhere else."

"I would have to agree. Best tell Conrad."

The drive home no longer feels tiring. Catalina moved in entirely a couple of months ago. She had to wait till her lease was up. She wouldn't let us pay it out for her. She also made us repaint the spare bedroom to a dark grey and told us the white looked out of place in the house. She isn't wrong, but it wasn't our fault. We never had a reason to paint or decorate that room. However, she turned it into a bedroom with a small art studio for herself, and I'm so proud of it. The odd time, she'll catch me in there admiring her artwork.

Nyx is graduating at the end of the school year. Then we don't have to hear him talk about how he has to study all the time. Dorian likes to remind him he wanted to stay in school. That only turns into a fight, so when that asshole walks across that stage, you bet your ass I'll be cheering the loudest because this house will feel less pressure.

"Think Cat will be home?"

"I don't think so. I think she finally went back to work in the cemetery. Davis called her last night to tell her the happy news."

"Still, she digs up bodies for the school, and no one has figured it out."

That one is still hard to think about, such a petite woman hauling bodies out of a hole. "Maybe we'll pop over and visit. Send her a message and find out where she is. I would say invite Nyx, but this makes him turn into a pussy."

The Eastwood Cemetery was never my favourite place to visit, yet I find myself here more than I thought I would. We swung home to switch vehicles. I know she doesn't want her car to be seen there, and Dorian wouldn't stop complaining. It turns out Nyx also wanted to come. If he barfs, I'll never let him forget it.

I spot her before she sees us. She's focused on digging that she has yet to look up once. No wonder it was easy for us to sneak up on her more than once, including this time.

"Little one, check your surroundings," I growl.

Her head snaps up, eyes round. Her bandana covers the lower half of her face, but I imagine her mouthing the words *fuck.*

She pulls it down, grimacing at us. "Will you guys stop sneaking up on me? I'm going to have a goddamn heart attack." She pushes her shovel into the dirt, walking to meet us.

"Hi, baby." Nyx plants a kiss on her lips. "Miss me?"

"Always, love."

Dorian wraps her in his arms, pulling her into a tight hug. "Half pint, how's it going so far?"

"Amazing, I'm so glad to be back out here." She kisses him as he lowers her to the ground.

She swung around to face me, smiling brightly. "And you, dickhole. My surroundings were fine five seconds ago. How the hell can you sneak up on me all the time?"

I lower my head to her ear, taking her earlobe between my teeth and pulling it lightly. She moans in frustration. "I have my ways, little one. Trust me."

"I hate when you call me that."

"No, you hate when I call you that because it makes you wet."

She closes her eyes, taking a deep breath. "I love you, Cole, but not right now. I'm dirty."

Dorian and Nyx laugh. She drops her head and groans.

"You said it, baby, not us," Nyx says, trying hard not to laugh more.

"I love you too, Wednesday."

1

NYX

Three years ago

The first year of college, and I have mixed feelings about it. Do I need a college education? Probably not, but what else am I supposed to do with my life? It's what's expected of me, and my parents want the best and only the best. I can't fail, or else my dad will be on my ass. I can't deal with him, and he's getting worse daily. I wanted to move in with Cole for school, and he quickly shot that idea down.

He also thinks Cole and Dorian are bad influences on me. He should know better. Dorian has been around since we were ten. I'm pretty sure he's not going to corrupt me. If anything, it's me that will be doing the corrupting.

The only thing he's worried about is me messing up his precious standings with the mayor. Like he doesn't know his fuckin' mayor is corrupt. That shady fuck is the worst of them all.

"Come on, man. We're hitting up the gang before school starts. It'll be fun." Cole stands in my room, arms crossed, looking like the asshole he is.

"The gang? Why would we head over to the Soul Stealers?" Dorian lays comfortably on my bed without a care to give.

"Because I have word they are looking for recruits. It would be perfect for us."

"To be honest, I wouldn't mind. I need to get out of this house."

Dorian sits up. "Getting that bad?"

I spin around in my chair, looking at him. "You don't even know. You are so lucky your grandmother doesn't helicopter over every move you make."

I'll admit, Dorian's grandmother is the coolest grandmother I've ever met.

"Move it. This is going to be great. The leader, Henry, is the guy to see about signing up if we want to."

I've never seen Cole this excited, except maybe the first time he got laid. I've never seen a smile on his face that reached his eyes before—that was years ago.

"We best hurry before my dad gets back. If he catches us, I'm toast."

"You know, we can always take care of him if you want." Dorian grins.

"What's the point? With our luck, it wouldn't work, and we'll get busted."

We all head downstairs, and this house is too stale for my liking. Mom has a habit of keeping things looking like a catalogue, and it's disturbing. Everything has a place, and she would know if I moved anything. I'm going insane being here. This family thinks they are all socialites, and they aren't. All because of fuckin' Coleman.

The Soul Stealers compound is entirely insane. A large bonfire burns in the middle of the parking lot with what looks like the entire gang around it. Everyone is embarrassing one another and laughing; it's a perfect family.

"This looks amazing." Dorian's voice lights up from the front seat.

"I told you." Cole gives him a smug look.

Great, he'll never let us forget about this.

"We need to find Henry, and he'll tell us everything we need to know before we make our minds up." Cole steers the car near all the others.

Music booms from somewhere in the distance, and adrenaline rushes through me. I've never been excited to do something behind my dad's back. He would never think twice about looking for me here. Dorian wraps his arm around my shoulder, giving me a slight jerk into his side.

"Let Cole have his fun. He seems relaxed here, and I've never seen him like this in a long time. Don't worry about your dad. I would love to see him come here with all these fine folks." He laughs.

"It's not so much him finding me. It's more when I get home that worries me."

"You could move out, and you are technically an adult now."

"I tried that. They said they would stop paying for my schooling if I did. It's so fucked."

Not that I want to be in school, but what else is there for me to do in this town? I can go to the EU, join the gang or move to the Southside. If my dad had his way, he would push me into politics.

As we near the fire, I watch Cole chat with an older man with dark hair, so this must be Henry. He turns and drinks his beer, watching Dorian and I close the gap.

"Henry, this is Dorian and Nyx." Cole introduces us. I reach out, shaking Henry's waiting hand.

"Good to meet you. What brings you by tonight?"

I nod in Cole's direction. "He pretty much dragged me out of the house and told us about you recruiting."

His eyes light up. "Well, I'll be damned. Three youngins want to join us. Follow me, and I'll introduce you to a few of the men and give you a rundown on how things are run around here."

All right, nothing seems sketchy so far. He introduces us to a few guys and tells us how the gang works and what would be expected from us. It looks like something I wouldn't mind trying. The only catch is—

"An enforcer? You want all three of us to be enforcers?" Dorian asked, brushing his fingers through his hair.

"I do. I think you guys would be perfect. Think about it." He heads back to the bonfire, leaving the three of us alone.

Cole stretches his arms sideways, spinning on his heels until he faces us. "I say we do this."

"Hold up. I think we should sleep on it. There is a lot to think about. Why don't we return to your place and relax a little." Dorian says as he starts walking to the car.

Cole follows him. "You wanna head back to my place? Why not yours?"

"Well, for one. My grandmother is there, and you have all the shit at your place."

"I'm down for that plan. I could go for a drink." This entire day is finally catching up, and I need to drown it out. Thank fuck it's Friday; there is no way I'm getting up tomorrow before noon.

"All right, fine. Luckily, that roomie of mine is gone. He's so annoying." Cole rolls his eyes before climbing behind the wheel.

"Cole, everyone is annoying to you," I tell him as I climb into the back seat.

"I can't help that. The world would be better if they weren't born with the stupid gene."

Oh, boy.

One thing about Cole is his attitude. He can't help himself. He always ends up ruining a good thing when his mouth opens up. Driving through Eastwood with the windows down and our music blaring, we are having the time of our lives. Dorian reaches under his seat, tossing back a mask. I grin at the style—Xs over the eyes and stitches over the mouth.

"Fuck going back to the dorm. Let's go to the Southside." I place the mask on, flicking the switch. The back of the car lights up green.

Cole places his mask on, lighting up in blue, and Dorian lights up in red. It's gonna be a good fuckin' night.

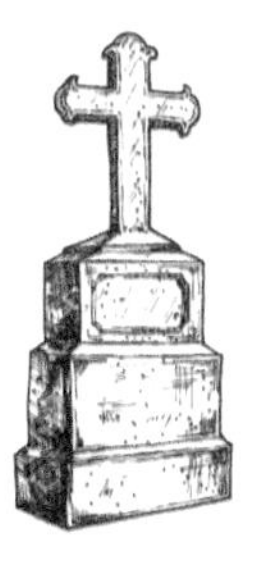

2

DORIAN

The Southside. You would never cross the tracks and come to this side if you were smart. The Soul Stealers aren't the only gang in town. If we joined them, we would have more control over this town. Maybe it wouldn't be a bad thing if we did. Henry seems like a decent guy.

We pull into a vacant parking lot, and every business is boarded up from the lack of support from the neighbourhood. More drug dealers are moving in and creating problems even on our side.

I face Cole. "You think the gang would be a smart move?"

He looks to Nyx and then back at me. "I think it would be good. Enforcers, though?" He furrows his brow and shrugs his shoulders. "That's a big job, and he wants us? We're nobodies. What does that say?"

"That we're either stupid or willingly ready to take the fall for this gang." Nyx shrugs.

"Only time will tell. Here, I have something to celebrate." Cole digs in his front pocket. Nyx groans.

"You have a joint? Where the fuck did you get that from?" I pluck it from his fingers. It's been a while since I've smoked. It's something I rarely do. I can tell by the way Nyx is acting, he's not excited at all.

"One puff won't kill you, bud." Cole lights up, taking a deep inhale before passing it to me.

God, I missed this. I swear it only took a second before my body felt like jelly. Grinning, I pass it to Nyx.

"I'm not sure about this."

"I won't push it on you, and it has to be something you want to try," I tell him. I will never push drugs on someone else. Either you want to do it, or you don't.

Nyx nervously takes the joint and stares at it before placing it between his lips. The first inhale, I can already tell it won't be good. Even Cole starts to laugh. Nyx coughs as smoke blows out of his mouth.

"Should've taken a smaller puff there, bud." Cole laughs.

"Fuck you," Nyx rasps. "You cunts never warned me about the burn." He coughs again, rubbing his throat.

"Smaller inhales this time." I watch as he does what I say. He passes it back to me before slumping in his seat.

"Give him a few. It'll be entertaining as fuck."

Oh, that it will be. Nyx needs this tonight. I feel sorry for the bastard. Small giggles fill the cab as it hits Nyx at once.

"Awe, man, I didn't even do that much. How come you two aren't laughing?"

"Because, young grasshopper, we are seasoned pros." Cole takes another puff.

Nyx laughs. It starts low in his chest before he falls over in his seat and bursts out loud. I shake my head, laughing along with him. I have to wipe my eyes from the tears that fall. Even Cole is laughing so much that he's crying.

"Shit, he's fucked." I press my hand on my aching ribs.

"We probably should get him home before his parents' return."

Nyx laughs again. "Fuck those parents. I don't need them."

Yep, he's done for the night. We better pray that his dad isn't home.

✦

The Thornton household always gave me the ick. The way Nyx's mom runs this house would've made me leave years ago. How he's kept sane is beyond me. Even the doormat is clean, not a speck of mud to be found. Nyx can't stop rolling around on the grass, pretending to make snow angels. I didn't think two puffs would affect him this much.

"Doooorian, the grass it's talking to me." He rubs his cheek deeper into the ground.

"No, bud, it's not." I shake my head, heading back in his direction. "Come on, up you go. Cole has the door open for us." I place my hands under his armpits, scooping him up. His brown eyes are bloodshot and unfocused; the next thing I know, his finger bops me on the nose.

His head falls backwards, and he bursts into laughter, stumbling back. I exhale slowly. It's like watching a toddler. Headlights illuminated the yard as they pulled into the driveway.

"Shit," Cole swore on his way over.

"Oh, no. Daddy's home!" the sarcasm dripping from his voice.

I have other words to use, but we'll go with his.

I watch Otis Thornton storm across the lawn, his face growing a lovely shade of scarlet with each step. I quickly grab Nyx, getting him standing and smacking his face.

"Smarten up. Your dad is on a rampage."

He sticks his tongue out and blows a raspberry. "I don't give a shit. Let Daddy-o come over." He snickers under his breath.

"What the fuck is going on? Out in public, of all things, Nyxon?" Otis grabs him out of my grip, shaking him. "Are you fucking stoned?"

"Are you fuckin' stupid?" Nyx leans into his dad's face.

A loud crack fills the air. Cole and I watch Nyx as tumbles onto his ass from the smack his dad landed on his cheek.

"You watch what you say to me, son." Otis squares his shoulders.

Cole goes to move, but I hold him back. "Don't," I whisper. "This needs to happen."

"Nyx is fucked up. It's not fair," Cole growled in his deep voice.

"Gonna beat me for all the neighbours to witness? That's one way to ruin the reputation you're trying to maintain, Daddy dearest." Nyx's tone mocked that of his dad.

Otis steps back. "No son of mine will be living in my house if he seeks the way of drugs."

Nyx scoffs. Getting to his feet, he moves forward. "It was one time. Don't act like I've done it multiple times. You can barely take a shit in that house without anyone knowing."

I advance closer. This conversation is getting heated, and if Otis tries anything, this is when he would. There are a few things that I'll put up with, but this isn't one of them.

"Otis, I think that's enough for tonight."

A mocking smile curled his lips. "Dorian, this isn't your place to say anything."

"No, but he's my friend, and I am going to look out for him. I'll bring him home tomorrow, and you two can talk about it when he's sober."

Otis doesn't say anything; he turns and walks away. The three of us stand there in silence, and I'm trying to figure out if he honestly kicked Nyx out for having done drugs once. It would be a little extreme if he did.

"I'll take you back to Dorians for the night, and we can figure this shit out in the morning," Cole says, turning and giving Otis one last glare before going to the car.

"You all right?"

Nyx storms toward the car. "I'm fine," he calls back.

He's anything but fine.

3

COLE

Things have taken a turn. I wasn't expecting shit to hit the fan last night with Nyx and his old man. You swear he was doing crack instead of smoking fuckin' weed. I never liked his dad; he came off with such an arrogant persona that I never cared for, even when I first met Nyx in grade eight.

Instead of having a chill Saturday, we are now helping Nyx pack his shit because no matter how much we all talked to Otis. It was a no-go to stay here. What a prick; he reminds me of my old man.

Nyx's mom didn't even try to stop any of this. All she did was sit back on that perfect cream couch and watch the entire argument go down. Makes me wonder if she even cares about her son.

"How the fuck am I supposed to pay for schooling, a place to rent and all the rest that I need?"

I toss his books in a box, trying to find an answer for him, only to come up with one solution. "Henry and the gang. What if we joined?"

"Seriously. Now's not the time for the gang bullshit, Cole." Dorian glares at me.

"Why not. It's perfect. We do a couple of jobs, get some money, and then we can move in together. I say we talk more with Henry and explain what happened."

"No, he's right. What could honestly go wrong? I'm already homeless if it's gonna shit on me, I'd rather it happen all at once." Nyx runs his hand through his hair, disappointment washing over his face.

He can think all he wants, and he isn't homeless. He's in between houses at the moment. Once we finalize everything with the Soul Stealers, things will start looking up for us.

Without a word, we all leave the house. Nyx loads the last box into the car before climbing into the backseat. There are so many things I want to say to him, but it wouldn't help him. Dorian shakes his head, not knowing what to say either.

We head for the compound first. The best thing to do is to get this conversation over with. If we aren't going to be a part of the gang, it's best to know right away. Then we can worry about plan B. I have no idea what that'll be; I'm banking on this to go through.

Freddy meets us at the door, arms crossed. "Can I help you, gentlemen?"

"Uh, we need to speak to Henry," I tell him, never taking my eyes off him. For an old man, he's built.

His grey eyebrow pops upwards. "Does he know you're all here?"

Nyx turns to me and cringes. "No. We wanted to talk about joining."

Freddy nods. "I hope you are prepared for everything that comes with it. It won't be easy initially, but it's like family here. If you ever need anything, don't be afraid to ask." He moves out of the way. "Henry is in the office. It's down the hall, past the bar."

"Thanks," we all say in harmony.

My heart is in my throat with sudden nerves. If I'm nervous about telling him we want to join, how the fuck am I supposed to be an enforcer. I know what enforcers do, and having nerves aren't allowed. Rounding the corner, Henry is already waiting for us.

"Welcome, boys, follow me. I had a feeling you would be back." He heads into his office.

Dorian narrows his eyes at him. "Don't. He didn't mean it like that."

"He better not. I'm not a boy," Dorian growls, pushing past me.

I stare at Nyx. His face twitches. "Stop. We can't start shit before we even get into the gang, Nyx," I warn him.

He closes his eyes, giving me a slight nod. "For now, but you know how Dorian is."

Don't we all? There's a reason why he was always with his grandmother growing up, and his parents couldn't be bothered to raise him. They didn't know what they were doing when they had him and spent most of their time yelling at him.

It gives me flashbacks to my childhood. I was lucky enough to get out, but living in foster homes wasn't how I saw myself growing up. I wish someone had gotten me out before the memories were engraved deep enough. The only thing Southside blessed me with was getting rid of my old man.

I can't say I'm proud to be where I'm from, but it's made me who I am today. I'll always place those that I love first. Dorian and Nyx are more than friends. They are my family, and I wouldn't be here today without them. I'll do anything for them, and I'm confident they would do anything for me.

We just have to get through this meeting.

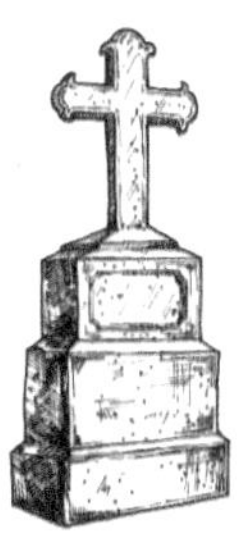

4

NYX

I can't believe we joined a gang. I'm not gang material. I'll be the first to admit Henry's rules are a little strange. The fact that he wants all of us to go to school is the weirdest. But he says he'll pay for it, which I'm grateful for since my asshole dad has officially cut me off.

If it wasn't for Dorian's grandmother, I would be homeless. That woman, I'm not sure how I'll ever make it up to her.

I'm lying in bed when Dorian and Cole come barging in so much for a relaxing time.

"What do you assholes want?"

Cole falls onto my bed next to me. "Henry called. He needs us at the compound in thirty."

Dorian moves over the top of us until he's beside the wall.

"Fuck, man, lay off the steroids." Cole reaches over me to shove Dorian.

"Don't blame my big bones that your skinny, you little prick."

Cole snorts. "You could only wish you were this skinny. What the fuck does your grandmother feed you?"

"Apparently, more than your shitty ass foster parents."

I hiss, trying to sink further into the mattress. I wait for a fist to fly.

"At least I can say the word *parent*. Where the fuck are yours?"

Sitting up, I raise my hands. "That's enough. All our parents are trash, end of conversation. What does Henry want us for?"

"Buzz kill," Cole mumbles.

I haul off, punching him in the shoulder. "Kill that, you cunt."

Dorian groans. "Speaking of killing, I hope you are ready to put your enforcing tasks to work."

I glance over my shoulder. "Henry wants us to kill someone?"

"Welcome to the gang life, Nyx."

When I signed up, deep down, this never crossed my mind. What can possibly go down in this town? The things you never knew or wanted to know. I liked living in the shadows, if my dad only knew what was happening in this town. His son doing drugs once wouldn't be the worst thing.

The directions are clear. Henry doesn't like competition. We need to take care of it, either make them listen or make it permanent. Henry doesn't care what we choose, but if this asshole doesn't listen, we'll be back out here.

Southside is Henry's number one competitor. It's funny if you think about it. Does he honestly think all the EU students would be coming out here for drugs? Most of those kids are too preppy for these roads. They would shit their pants if they crossed that line.

Playing with my mask, the adrenaline is already rushing through my body. I didn't think it would feel like this, but maybe Cole was right. Joining the gang is what we all needed. I have enough built-up frustration that I need an outlet, and somebody's face is precisely what I need.

Cole wants to keep our identity covered for now, hence the masks. I don't blame him; we don't need a target painted this early in the game. We aren't even sure if we are staying in Soul Stealers. That's all I need, is to walk down the street and be gunned down. At least this way, no one knows who we are until our reputation is built. Between Cole and Dorian, I don't think many will mess with us, I'm not the best fighter, but fuck, if it calls for it, I'll lay them out.

Dorian drives while Cole checks his gun for the tenth time. Out of all of us, he's the one that was born for this.

He may look like a preppy model douche, doesn't mean I want to cross him. Behind those baby blues lies a devil.

Cole sits sideways in his seat. "Once we get there, it will be a nut house. Henry probably wants a bullet in the guy's head."

"So guns a blazzin' is what you are saying," I confirm.

"Unless Dorian wants to blow the house up." Cole shrugs.

The corner of Dorian's mouth lifted. "I'm not opposed to that idea. Be quick, I packed the explosive."

"Of course you did."

Dorian grins at me through the rearview mirror. "Can't help myself."

The further we get into the area, the shittier the houses become. Every home should be torn down and this side of town forgotten. That would take a miracle. Coleman banks on this side for votes to stay in power. He's such a sleazeball.

We creep closer to our destination, and my heart finally gets the burst of adrenaline it needs. Reaching under my seat, I grab my gun. Henry gifted each of us a Desert Eagle for all of our jobs. I'm still not sure how to feel about it. Beating someone with my fist, yes.

But shooting someone? I'm still on the fence.

"Ready for this?" Dorian pulls the SUV over.

The drug house is down the block. People coming and going like the lion isn't hunting them. When a shiny Cadillac pulls up, we know shit's about to get real.

"This must be the big buyer. Should we hold back and see who it is?" I question, moving between the front seats to get a better look.

Cole leans forward, waiting for the driver to exit. "Who do we know drives a Caddy?"

There's only one name that comes to mind. "Coleman." I scoff. "What a piece of shit. No wonder he won't do anything about this side of town."

"Not like profiting off the poor even more." Dorian shakes his head. "I say we go in there and take care of Coleman too."

"You know we can't do that. We'll be charged with murder, without a doubt. We wait until he leaves, then take care of these pricks." I wonder what goes through his head some days. Nope, I take that back. I don't want to know anything in that pea brain of his.

Twenty minutes later, Coleman walks out, accompanied by none other than our dealer. If we're being honest, I can't remember his name. It won't be important come morning, anyway. The SUV is so quiet I can hear my heartbeat—every thump pulses through me.

"Get ready. The moment he pulls away, we move. Fuck the nice talk. If he's in bed with Coleman, this cunts a deadman." Cole doesn't look away from the front window as he speaks. "I suspect at least ten men inside—take them all out. Dorian can burn it down after."

The Desert Eagle feels like a thousand pounds in my hand. If I want to stay in the gang, I'll have to prove myself one way or another. In a matter of seconds, we are exiting the SUV and running across the street. The closer we get, the louder the house becomes.

"Masks on, when I reach three, storm in. Don't ask questions, and don't fuckin' die." Cole pulls his mask on, looking the part.

Dorian and I pull our masks down and stand beside Cole, waiting for the show to start.

"One... Two." He cocks his gun.

Cocking my gun, Cole advances on the front of the house, fucker could never count fully. Whoever was milling around on the steps caught sight of us, drawing their weapons.

"Who the fuck are you assholes, stepping up on us?" one prick speaks. He moves to the edge of the steps.

Cole laughs, aiming his gun. "Your worst nightmare." Pulls the trigger, shooting him in the chest.

Gunshots ring out.

Taking the back way behind the house, I plan to cut off anyone trying to escape over the fence and into the alley. Things are going a mile a minute; it's like a scene from a movie, not like being thrown into stuff from the get-go.

"Nyx, he's coming out of the house," Cole yells from behind me.

Quickly turning, we find our drug dealer making his escape. He can run, but he won't make it very far. I catch up to him, running into him.

"Where the hell do you think you are running off to, you chicken shit?" Pointing my gun at his head.

He snickers. "You're just a child. What are you gonna do?"

All that pent-up frustration that didn't get used on my dad comes to the surface. My fist lands a loud blow to the cunts face. The pain is welcoming. Especially when the drug dealer hollers in pain.

"Fuckin' pussy. If you can deal the drugs, you can deal with the pain," I barked in his face. "Your operation is over with. I send regards from the Soul Stealers."

He covers his face. "No, please," he begs. "I'm just an errand boy. Don't you want the bigger fish?"

"Tell me who, and I won't shoot you." Pulling the gun away a little, waiting for him to answer.

He turns his head, eyes widen. My head barely turns before Cole shoots his gun. Blood splatters all over my shirt and mask.

Jumping back, I rip my mask off. "What the fuck, Cole! I almost had more information out of him."

"We don't have time for small talk, Nyx. Shoot, don't talk."

It wasn't small talk, you asshole. It would've been something to take back to Henry, a guaranteed stay in the gang. It would've been a big win if we took down the big man. Leave it to Cole to be trigger-happy.

"Come on, before you get shot." Dorian pats me on the back.

I shrug him off. "I almost had it, D." Closing my thumb and finger together. "This fuckin' close, and he ruined it all."

He lifts his mask onto his head. "There will be another chance, Nyx. It's our first job. We can't always go in full force."

They wouldn't understand. If this doesn't work out, I'd lose a lot. My entire life is riding on being in Soul Stealers. I'm not sure what my future would look like without it.

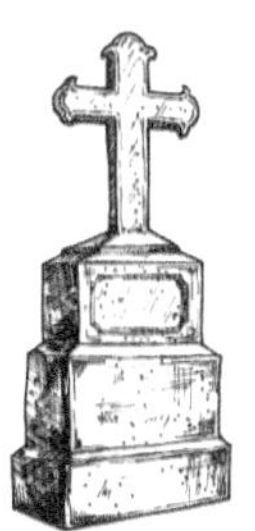

5

COLE

"Cole, this is a bad idea, and you know it." Dorian glares at me from across the kitchen table.

I give him a double shrug. "I know it is. You know it is. But it needs to be done."

"Have you told Nyx?"

"About that." I play around with my coffee cup, deflating the question.

"You idiot. He's going to find out, and it probably should be from one of us."

Rubbing my temples, I meet his green eyes. "No shit. Give me some time. I'll do it."

He chuckles. "Wanna pinkie promise?" He asks, wiggling his finger at me.

I'll figure out a time to tell him; he doesn't have to know now. We technically have two weeks before things go to hell. So, in all honesty, I have a week.

The front door crashes open, making both Dorian and I jump. He raises a brow, and I internally cringe; whatever happened can't be good. Nyx storms into the kitchen seconds later, covered in dirt and grease.

"Don't ask." He grunts on his way to the sink.

I'm gonna say his bike is acting up again. There are better times to tell him the news.

"Cole has some news for you," Dorian spits out.

"What the fuck?" I said, spreading my arms wide in disbelief. He threw me under the fuckin' bus.

Nyx turns to me. "What is it? It better be good."

I nod in the direction of the empty chair. This is definitely a sit-down conversation. I wait for him to finish washing his hand and to sit before dumping this shit on him. I would've carried it around longer if I could, but Dorian is right. He needs to know, and I should be the one to tell him.

"Spill it, Cole. I have shit to fix."

"All right, fine. Henry got word from the mayor that purge night is a go this year."

"Nope, not doing it." He pushes his chair out.

I hold my finger up, freezing his actions. "We don't have a choice. The mayor is running for office again this year, and he thinks that he'll get another term if he does another purge night."

Nyx scoffs, rolling his eyes. "That's the stupidest shit I've ever heard. Why do we always have to get sucked into politics? This is bullshit. How are we going to protect the town and Cat?"

"Well, for one. Half pint is not leaving this house on Halloween," Dorian states.

No fuckin' shit.

"Conrad also suggested that we—"

Nyx holds his hand up. "Nope, that's enough. I'm not having it."

"Listen to him, Nyx. It's important."

"You think handling club business for a town that doesn't give a shit about us is important? Get off that high horse, Dorian. The only reason I'm still in that stupid club is because of you, two."

I should've seen this coming. "We don't have a choice. We do what Henry tells us. You know the rules."

"The rules didn't help us when we needed them."

With that, he storms out of the kitchen.

"Well, that went better than I thought, to be honest. I'm sure he'll come around. We have a week before we have to figure shit out, anyway." Dorian shrugs.

"Glad you're the optimistic kind. I'm not sure he will be this time around. Henry really fucked him over."

"I'm headed out. Let me know when half pint gets home."

I wave him off, then head downstairs. I need to blow off some steam, and unfortunately, I don't have anyone to torture, so my body will have to suffice. Pulling my shirt off and tossing it onto the bench, I head over to the abused punching bag. I'm sure we could buy a new one, but this one is well-loved. If you overlook the duct tape layers, it still works perfectly.

My gloves sit off to the side; I would wear them any other day, but today, I need to feel some pain. Henry is driving me up the wall with all this mayor bullshit.

The first hit is a welcoming feeling. I also hate how Conrad has weaselled his way so far into everything that he thinks he's now King of Turd Island. I land another punch, the worst thing about the mayor's newest idea. He wants Purge Night to be bigger and better than last year. Surrounding towns got wind of it after he met with all the mayors. He wanted more people to enjoy it.

Because that's what Eastwood fuckin' needs.

I swear our mayor is so detached from reality it's unreal. How he keeps getting voted back in blows me away. That should tell you how many people enjoy having him in the office to get this one night of the year.

I hammer harder and faster into the bag, sweat pouring down my back. I'm so far into my head that I never noticed somebody else had come down here.

"I would say you look hot, but what the fuck Cole?" Cat shakes her head. "Wanna explain to me why you didn't glove up?"

I can't help but give her a smirk. Her black hair is gathered up in a messy bun, and what I wouldn't do to tear that oversized sweatshirt off her. Those goddamn thigh highs only lead to what I want the most.

"Cole, upstairs now." She snaps her fingers, pointing to the stairs.

She's been cockblocking me for days now. This wasn't supposed to happen when moving your girlfriend in. She's driving me up the wall walking around wearing shit that shows off her ass. She does it on purpose.

And to add more to the fire, I follow her up the stairs, and I swear she adds more swing to her step.

"Sit. I'll get the first aid kit."

I give my hands a flex. They aren't that bad—bleeding, yes. But they could be worse.

"Here, place this on them. It'll help with the swelling. What the hell were you thinking, anyway?" She passes me an ice pack and sets up her little station on the kitchen table.

"I have a lot of shit going on, Wednesday. It was the bag or some asshole that I would come across on the street with."

Her violet eyes swept me up and down. "What's going on, Cole?"

"It's club business, so don't be telling anyone, got it?"

She rolls her eyes. "Who the fuck would I tell? The next dead body I dig up?" She grabs the antiseptic spray and then holds my right hand.

"You could've made a friend with Riley if you wanted to. We weren't stopping you."

Shrugging her shoulder. "I know. I guess I don't know how to make friends, and what am I supposed to do with him? I have enough guys in my life already." She chews on her lip.

"Wednesday." My fingers trace her chin as my thumb pulls her lip free. "Stop being hard on yourself. If you want friends, make them. If you don't, that's fine too. But think about making one with Riley."

"Fine, don't think this worked from telling me what's happening with your little squad." Her little black eyebrow pops up.

"You better sit."

She backs away. "Shit, it's bad, isn't it. What has Henry done now?"

I pull her into me. "It's not like last time." I drop my head on her stomach. "The mayor wants to bring back purge night." Her hands run through my hair.

"What does that mean, exactly?" She tugs my head back.

"I mean, he's running for mayor again and wants a guaranteed vote back into the office. He wants a more phenomenal purge night than last year. Our job is to make sure it goes off without a hitch."

"It's gonna be worse, isn't it?"

I nod. "I think so. Dorian and I are concerned, but Henry doesn't seem to care."

"And Nyx?"

I take a deep breath before letting it out. "Cat. Things with Nyx and Henry are complicated, and I don't see them patching things up soon. But Nyx needs to realize that this is a job, and he has to do it without bitching. No one is thrilled about this, but we don't have a choice."

"When?"

"Like always, on Halloween night, he wants surrounding towns involved. We don't want you going out anywhere."

She steps back, crossing her arms. "Cole, don't start with me. I'm sure I can handle making my own choices, and besides, I learnt last year to stay inside on purge night because masked assholes hang around the cemetery."

I chuckle. "Yeah?" Moving toward her, I curl one hand around her neck and my other on her hip. "I'm pretty sure you love having those masked assholes around."

I watch as she licks her lips, sending my body into overdrive. I've had enough of her tormenting me. This ends now; lifting her, she wraps her legs around my waist. I move us to the kitchen table.

"I've had enough of you ignoring me, and I want what I want, little one."

She presses her heels into my back, pushing me closer. "Yeah, what do you want, Cole?" she asks, pulling up her sweater, showing off a pair of Halloween underwear.

I slowly slide my fingers up her thigh, watching her skin prickle with goosebumps. "I could spend all day looking at this pussy, little one." I slip off her underwear, getting a good look at her wet and waiting pussy. "Wanna know what I want?"

"Yeah," she whispered, her eyes craving with passion.

I move my hand to my jeans, unsnapping them. Slipping my hand inside, my cock is already dripping for her. My pants dip below my ass, exposing my cock to her.

"Mmm, I'll never get tired of seeing that." Her gaze lands on my piercing.

I give myself a nice long stroke, and when I flick the piercing, it makes my cock grow harder. God, I can't wait to sink deep inside of her. Lining up, I smack her clit with my cock.

"I need you so bad right now, and this is what you get for making me wait. You're not going to come. This is your punishment." I drive into her with abrupt force, making her scream. Her body slides up the table. I have to pull her back into me. My fingers flex into her thighs, and I can't help but watch my cock disappear into her.

"Cole, I need you deeper."

"You'll take what I give you." I withdraw all the way, only to enter slowly until the head of my cock disappears again. I watch as her fingers work toward her clit. "Not so fast, I told you. You aren't coming." I wrap my hand around her wrist, raising it above her head. I reach down, grabbing her other wrist and restraining her.

I capture her mouth before slamming back into her hard. Her fingernails dig into the back of my hand, making me pound into her faster. Her little whimpers edge me further. The thought of her not getting to finish is my undoing.

"Fuck, little one." I drop my head into her neck, spilling everything inside her. "Fuck, I love you."

"Yeah, well, I hate you."

"That's because you're mad. Trust me, when Nyx comes back, he'll appreciate it." Kissing her neck, I slip out of her, watching my cum leak out of her. "That's a sight I'll never get tired of."

"This is why I cut you off all the time, dickwad." She half laughs, jumping off the table.

I fuckin' believe that. I may be hard to deal with, but it's not my fault. It's how I was raised.

"Don't get angry with me. This is your fault."

"Don't push your luck."

She narrowed her eyes at me, and I would be scared, but the last time she tried to hurt me, she only ended up hurting herself. I'll never let that happen again.

6

DORIAN

I thought we were done with all this bullshit.

All Henry is doing is feeding into the mayor and giving what he wants. He's nothing but an enabler, and they both need to be stopped. If I have anything to do with it, this will be the last year for the purge. Throughout the entire drive, all I see are Coleman for Mayor signs. I had to refrain myself from running each one over. I respect my bike too much for that.

Pulling into the grocery store parking lot, I can already feel myself getting mad. I knew I should've just done online pickup. But they always fuck up my order and substitute my items with the most random things. If I want a potato, don't tell me I want a litre of milk instead. Those things are in different departments.

No one else in the house has figured out cooking besides Cat. Between the both of us, we feed the house, but when we aren't home. The boys starve. It's not that hard to make a simple dish, fuck spaghetti is easy. I guess not everyone had a loving grandmother like I did. I miss her so much.

The stares I get walking up and down the aisle should annoy me, but I ignore them. Some are less keen on a biker club in town. It's no different from a gang, except for the cut I now wear every time I leave the house. It doesn't help that our logo is a giant skull with a scythe.

Every mom grabs their kid like I'm gonna snatch them and take them back to my perv van. If they only knew that we help find the dirty fuckin' pervs in this town. We do everything we can in the club to keep this town safe, then one night a year, it gets flushed down the drain.

You might as well call us hypocrites.

The whispers only grow louder the longer I take. If people think my shopping in the grocery store is controversial, just wait until the mayor drops his bombshell soon. Then we'll see who the bad guy really is in this town. All I want is for Cat to graduate then we can move away.

I'm almost at the checkout when I bump into somebody. Turning, I come face to face with Conrad. Great.

"Fancy running into you here." Conrad grins.

"Well, it is a grocery store in a small town. What do you expect?" Just because he's my VP doesn't mean jack shit.

His lips twitch. "Don't be like that. Henry told me you aren't excited about this Halloween."

Loosey lips Linda I see. Henry never could keep shit to himself.

"This is your first year here, Conrad. That's the only reason you're excited. Give it time, a few hours in, and you'll be over it, too. The only ones that benefit from it are the ones that have a fantasy about chasing women in the fuckin' park."

That doesn't sound good when I think about it, considering we chased Catalina last year. But that's different, we knew what we were doing, and it wasn't a sick fuckin' fantasy. And she wasn't a one-night thing.

"Either way, you need to be prepared too, Dorian. You are an enforcer for the club."

"Yeah, I'm well aware of my fuckin' job." Moving away, I move back in line. Fuck him. It's none of his concern about my life unless I have club business to handle.

I think we are still stuck in the mentality of a gang, and it's hard to transition from one mindset to another.

I always get excited seeing Cat's black Volkswagen in the driveway. I guess it was too much for Cole to shoot me that text. The sight of our house never gets old either, when Cat moved in, she made it her mission to plant a flower bed, and of course, she had to keep the dark theme. I never realized how many flowers come in deep shades of purple, black or dark red. It's beautiful, I'll admit, and I'm not a flower guy.

Climbing off my bike, I grab the groceries from the saddlebags. The neighbourhood is already starting to look perfect for fall; the leaves are changing, and the smell of fall is in the air. In no time, decorations will be out; I feel most sorry for those who don't decorate.

They'll be targeted first when the purge starts. The younger teens always vandalize buildings because they know the cops won't do anything to them.

There's only one rule: no murder. And shockingly, it's never been broken.

I'm barely in through the front door, and it's chaos.

"What the fuck do you want from me?" Nyx throws a pillow at Cole.

"I want you to fuckin' man up and do what's expected from you."

I spot Cat out of the corner of my eye, standing at the edge of the kitchen, shaking her head. I slowly make my way over to her.

Lowering my head, I whisper, "What's going on?"

She releases a sigh. "Nyx wants out of the club, to be honest. I think it was the wrong move to let him stay. He should've stayed out."

I walk the rest of the way into the kitchen, placing the bags on the counter. As the yelling continues, I pack the food away.

"Dorian, aren't you going to break them up?"

"No, darling. That is one fight that needs to happen. Cole can't always get his way. He needs to listen to others for once, I tried to tell him that Nyx wanted out, but he wouldn't listen. I think the final push for Nyx was Henry fucking him over."

She walks over to me, wrapping her arms around my waist. "That's low and horrible. If you make a promise, the most you can do is keep it."

I tip up her chin. "Some things are meant to be learnt the hard way." I lower my lips above hers, slowly inching my tongue until it touches hers. Her mouth opens, inviting me in. Running my hand through her hair, I hold her still. Swiping my tongue against hers before closing my mouth, feeling her lips move with mine.

A loud crash comes from the living room before I can feel her body closer.

"Fuck."

"I told you to deal with them," amusement dripped from her voice.

"Watch it, half pint. I'm not their parent. The only person I'm going to punish around here is you."

She licks her lips and slowly rakes her eyes down my body. With a grin, she spins around and heads into the living room.

Goddamn her. When I walk into the living room, it's a mess. Pillows are thrown all over the floor, everything on the coffee table is scattered along the floor, and my eyes travel to the broken glass where Cat is standing.

She gently picks up the broken frame that held a picture of herself and her dad, and my heart breaks. As much as she didn't talk to her dad, I knew she loved him.

"Shit, baby. I'm sorry." Nyx reaches for her, crushing her close to his chest. "We didn't mean to break it, I swear."

"Let me go, Nyx."

He lets go, slowly backing away. I turn to Cole, a mournful look outfitted him. Good, I hope he finally fuckin' learnt a lesson.

"Wednesday?"

"Don't, Cole. Why can't you two deal with your shit without breaking other people's things? I'll be in the kitchen making supper if you need me."

I reach out to her, but she brushes me off. Turning back to the two assholes.

"What the fuck? Why do you always insist on starting shit for the sake of starting it, Cole? Can't you just leave it alone?"

"What do you want me to do?" Cole gets in my face. "I'm only trying to do what's best."

"For who? You or him?"

"For everyone," he spits out. "Why can't you think about everyone else for once."

I shake my head in disbelief. "What do you think I've been doing?" I point to Nyx. "He made up his mind, end of story. After Halloween, he's out. You got that?" I glance over at Nyx, who has been quiet the entire time.

"I can deal with everything until after Halloween. Sorry about the mess. I'll clean it up."

I wait until Nyx leaves before saying what I want to say.

"Cole, I'm worried about him. He's not the same since Henry fucked him over."

I watch him take a deep breath, kicking a pillow across the floor. "I know. It did a number on him. It fucked with his trust issues, and I'm unsure how to help him. I thought keeping him in the club would be the cure, but I was wrong. It's only made things worse. Every day, his demons are coming out."

"Perhaps what needs to be done is for him to get out. Only two weeks, and it's over. We'll tell Henry in the morning."

"Yeah, okay. We'll call a meeting and get it over with. I'm sure Conrad will have a field day with this."

Conrad can kiss my ass for all I care. He has no say in what happens until Henry leaves or dies. His opinion does not matter. Nyx deserves so much more than being in this club—everyone knows it.

"You need to go in there and apologize to Cat. A real one, Cole, not your bullshit ones that you always do."

"Whatever, asshole." He storms into the kitchen.

He was doing so well, but a tiger cannot change his stripes, and I shouldn't expect Cole to be a nice guy.

7

CATALINA

I knew something was the matter with Nyx, yet no one would help him. His downward spiral has me worried. I want the fun, happy-go-lucky Nyx back. I miss him. But he's been gone for months now. This club has been sucking the life out of him, I'm not sure what the difference is between the club and the gang, but he needs to talk to me. Because fighting between everyone clearly isn't helping.

I slam down the pasta sauce, getting frustrated with the entire situation. Cole doesn't help things either, and he always has to act like the boss. For once, he can consider other people's feelings.

"Wednesday? Can I talk to you outside?" Cole's deep voice interrupts my ranting thoughts.

I don't bother answering him. Turning away from him, I head for the door that leads to the backyard. I continue walking until I'm halfway across the yard. I stand there facing the fence, breathing heavily, becoming more pissed off by the second. Cole's large hand lands on my forearm, spinning me around.

"Look at me, please. I'm not talking to your back."

His blue eyes pierce into mine. "The back is all you deserve right now, Cole. I can't believe you guys."

"One last job, and then he's out, I promise."

I laugh, shaking my head in disbelief. "Yeah, does Nyx know this?"

"He does. He agreed to it." He moves his hand down my arm, squeezing my fingers. "Listen. I'm sorry about your photo. Things got out of hand, and I didn't mean to ruin anything of yours. We shouldn't have fought like that."

"No shit. You idiots always do this. I'm getting tired of it, Cole. I'm not sure if I can take much more of it if I'm being completely honest."

I watch as his face crumbles. "Wednesday," he whispered in a rough texture. "What do you mean?"

I look at a dead spot on the grass. His finger lifts my chin, meeting my eyes. "Tell me, please, are you leaving me?"

"Cole, I don't know what you want me to say."

"I want you to say you won't leave when things get tough."

I hold my finger up, shutting him up. "When things get tough. Are you kidding me? Do you think this little fight you and Nyx had is when things get tough? Are you shitting me right now?" I don't have to remind him what happened last year.

He tilts his head to the sky. "That's not what I meant." His eyes collide with mine.

"Then explain because the hole is only getting deeper."

He spins around, facing the house. "Fuck, Catalina. I don't know what I mean. I'm shit for words, and you know this."

And this is the problem. He won't express himself, and he refuses to open up. I don't know why. I only want to understand him better. After all this time, I hardly know him.

"I accept your apology, but I have supper to make." I brush past him, heading inside. I won't leave them, especially over a fight. But I swear if they can't figure their shit out fast, I'm unsure how much more I can take. It's taking a toll on me.

"You okay, darling?" Dorian asks as soon as I enter the kitchen.

"I'm not sure, and everything is so fucked I'm not sure what to do anymore." I drop my head into my hands, my entire body slumping forward.

Dorian wraps his arms around me, pulling me tight against his chest. "Stop. You don't need to worry about anything that happens in the club. It's club business, and it never should've entered the house. I'm sorry that we did this to you, Cat."

"It's not your fault, it's my fault. I gotta stop asking for details and stick to what I know best."

He steps back and grins. "Yeah, what's that?"

"Dead bodies."

"Oh, half pint. That's one reason why I love you so much. Let's forget about this and start supper."

He presses a kiss to my forehead before turning back to the stove.

Maybe he's right. Perhaps the club shit should stay out of the house, but when it starts to affect one of them, I can't help but get worried. These are my men—anything that happens to them happens to me.

Nyx walks in with the broom and dustpan. "I'm sorry, baby."

"I don't blame you, Nyx. I don't blame any of you."

"Well, you should. This entire thing is a fucking shit show!" he yells. His chest rose and fell on ragged breaths.

My heart breaks. Things were going so great up until Henry. Is it rude for me to think about digging up his body one day? So the students can examine what a piece of shit he truly is. Fuckin' karma is gonna come after me hard for that thought.

I watch Nyx walk away. This entire house is falling apart, and I don't know how to fix it.

"Half pint, let him cool down. Come, eat before you head to work."

He brings our supper to the table, setting it down.

"What cemetery are you at tonight?"

"Eastwood one."

Dorian cups my face, lowering his close to mine. "Please be safe. This time of year, everyone gets stupid."

I bring my hands to his. "I will, and I have the Bluetooth earbud, so if anything goes wrong, I can call you. I'll be safe, I promise."

"Don't make promises, half pint."

With a quick kiss, I pull out of his hands. "Don't be such a worried wart. No one hangs out in the cemeteries except loners, remember."

"Don't. You aren't a loner. Did you want me to come with you?"

"Nah, I think I need some peace for a while."

With a smile, he finally sits.

The medical department parking lot is vacant when I pull in. Even Dr. Deadbodies is gone. He's probably on his date with Professor Adams. I knew something was up when I saw Davis come into class out of the blue. Now, I hardly see him around the medical department.

I'm glad to be out of the house tonight. The guys need to get their shit sorted out without me being a referee.As much as I love them, I need some alone time.

The silence of the cemetery will be welcomed.

Parking next to the van, I grab my bag from the back seat along with the blue tooth earbuds from the ashtray. The guys would be pissed if I didn't have these with me. Ever since my stupid asshole of a brother kidnapped me, they've been overly protective of me heading out at night. I won't lie, I've been nervous ever since.

I have to remind myself that I'm no longer in danger and can't keep living in fear. I'm taking all the precautions I can, and Cole even taught me a few self-defence moves. Not that I'm any good, but it'll be good for what I need. One good kick to the nuts will give me enough time to run.

I need to dig up three bodies tonight, and I'm glad they are all in the same cemetery. Not that going out to Eaglewood is terrible; the travelling is killing me lately, especially when Dr. Deadbodies fills my night with both cemeteries.

I think it's his way of getting back at me for being taken by dickhead Conrad.

The weather is warm tonight, not unusual for this time of year, but it also brings out clear skies. Clear skies are also my worst nightmare. The way the moon is out illuminating the area too much, giving me away; I need to be extra observant.

I pull the van as close as I can to the far end of the road. Being by the woods still sends chills down my spine.

"Grow the fuck up, Cat," I mumble to myself.

I stare into the woods, waiting for a shadow figure to jump out. This overactive mind will be the death of me. When I think no one is watching me, I head to the back of the van, where all my equipment is. Nyx suggested I get a little wagon to haul everything back and forth. But I think it would be more of a hassle in the end. I've been doing it this way for so long that I know how it works.

Counting the rows, I finally come across the grave Davis told me about. It's not the freshest, so I'll be digging for a while. I can only hope it's not a heavy body. Riley has been working overtime in the lab; with the cooler weather coming next month, we both will be inside again. I'll admit it was nice working with him, but I was glad to be outside once spring had arrived.

I stare at the grave and the packed-down dirt. Sweet fuckin' Jesus, this is gonna take me hours to get to the coffin. Shoving the shovel into the ground, I drop the rest of my supplies.

Releasing a deep sigh, I get to work.

The resounding thunk of the shovel hitting wood brings me sweet relief. I can hardly hold on to the shovel as my arms scream in pain. My lungs are on fire as I slump over the shovel handle, trying to catch my breath.

That's it. I'm telling Davis only fresh graves from now on.

I don't even think I can climb out of this hole, and here I figured I was on my game with all the workouts I was getting in. But I can't stay in this hole all night. Willing my body to work, I reach for the grass at the tip of the hole.

When someone's fingers touch mine, I stumble backward. I shut my eyes tightly when thoughts of my brother staring down at me wearing the yellow lite-up mask and memories of what happened last year race through my mind. Fear chases over my skin like an icy wave, my mind going completely blank.

"Baby," Nyx whispered in my ear, his head burrowed into the hollow of my neck as he pulled me closer to his chest. "I won't let you slip into those memories. Breathe for me, baby. I need you here with me and only with me. Listen to my breathing and match it. Okay?"

I try with all my might to focus on his breathing. No matter what I do, flashes of him standing over me won't leave.

"Cat, it's only you and I."

I focus on Nyx's words and less on my thoughts. No one is here to hurt me, and I'm past all that now.

"I'm here. It's only you and I," I repeat.

"That's right, baby. How about we get out of this hole now, okay?"

I wait until he climbs out first to take a deep breath finally.

8

NYX

Being a university graduate, I thought it would bring me more opportunities, but apparently, I should've chosen a better career because taking all those bullshit classes did little for me. I'm still stuck in the Soul Stealers.

Henry acts like he's the ruler of my life. Little does he know, no one rules my life except for me. I'm out of this club after Halloween, if he likes it or not. I can't be around somebody that goes against their word. I can't trust him after the hell he put me through a couple of months ago. And he is now doing the mayor's bidding to further his lifestyle. I can't be a part of that either.

If I think about it any longer, I'm gonna lose my god-damn mind. I need to escape from this house, and being around Cole isn't helping. He doesn't understand what I'm going through. He only has his mind set on one thing; unfortunately, it's not what everyone else wants. His head is so far up his ass he forgets about the world and everyone in it.

There is only one spot I can think of that will help me calm down. Without a word, I leave the house. Climbing onto my bike, I rev my engine before taking off down the road. The wind feels wonderful on my skin. It's what I needed after fighting with Cole.

I let the road take me to my destination. The cemetery is quiet this late at night. I've been coming here since finding Catalina here last year. It's an excellent place to clear your head; no one is here to talk to you.

The moon gleams across the path on my way to the back of the cemetery. Noticing Cat's van parked, I park beside it and listen to where she is. In the distance, I can faintly hear the shovel crunching through the dirt.

As I near the hole, I notice her hand reaching the edge. Without thinking, I grab it to help her up. I didn't even think about what happened to her last year. My brain fuckin' glitched.

"Shit, shit, shit."

I quickly jump into the gravesite, pulling her into my chest. I do everything I can to pull her out of those horrible memories. She takes a deep breath by the time we get out of that goddamn hole.

"I'm so sorry, baby. I wasn't thinking," I apologize again.

She shakes her head. "Don't apologize. You didn't do anything wrong."

I cup her face, lowering mine to hers. "Listen to me. I should've known better. God, baby, I'm so sorry."

She whispered in a low, raspy voice, "It's not your fault, Nyx. I didn't expect to have that kind of reaction, that's all. Why, after all this time, does he still get that reaction from me?"

I stroke the back of her head, trying to give her reassurance. I have nothing to say because what can I say? Besides, give it time. Time doesn't heal all fuckin' wounds.

"Did you want to stay and help me with this body?"

I grimace. "Yeah, sure."

She backs up, laughing. "It's not that bad."

"Cat, my stomach is already turning. I don't get how you can do this every night and not be yacking in the bushes."

She pats her stomach and gives me a grin. "Made of steel, baby."

I blow out a breath, steel. That's what I need. I watch as she grabs the hooks from the tarp and walks to the grave's edge.

"I'll hook all this up if you want to haul the body up. I'm still too tired from digging."

"Yeah, I can do that."

She shakes her head before lowering down. My girl is the strongest person I know and never gives up. No matter what gets thrown at her, she still pushes forwards.

I help load the body into the back of the van, slamming the door shut.

"Did you wanna talk about earlier today?" Her violet eyes settle on me with concern.

"Not really, there isn't anything to talk about. It is what it is. I'm leaving after Halloween, and Henry can do whatever he needs to. I'm tired of it all. I should've left months ago."

Her warm fingers brushed the side of my face. "Nyx. You didn't know Henry was going to do that."

I turn away. "I should've seen it coming." I'm so disappointed in myself.

"Love. How were you to know he would cut your school finances off and then tell the Dean that you were responsible for everything?"

"Because when I signed up, he was all 'Education is number one'. What fuckin' bullshit. If he didn't care, then why get my hopes up. I almost lost everything." I slam my fist into the side of the van, breathing hard. I'll never forgive Henry for what he did. He knew how much going to school meant to me. It was an escape; no matter how much I didn't like going, I needed it. I needed to get out of my head and drown myself in those books.

Cat's hand lands on my shoulder, and I quickly wrap my hand around her waist, slamming her into the van.

"I just wanted to comfort you. You comforted me when I needed it."

Pushing her leggings down, rubbing my finger on her clit, getting her wet. Her sweet moans fill the quiet night air.

"I fucking need you more than I need to breathe right now."

She grips my forearm tight. "Nyx, I need more, please." She tilted her head back, exposing her neck.

I reach up, gripping her neck, watching her eyes flutter shut. I've always loved how her body responds to my touch. Her hand dips into my jeans, finger brushing against the tip of my dick. Brushing my lips alongside her jaw, working my way to her ear.

"I wanna hear you scream, wake the dead, baby," I whisper.

I turn her around, bending her over. She flattens her hands on the side of the van, pushing her ass out further. Yeah, she already knows what I'm after. Popping the button on my pants, I unzip just enough to pull my dick out. Running my fingers along the back of her thigh, I watch as her skin pebbles.

"Fuck, I love you, Catalina."

She peers over her shoulder, giving me a gentle smile. "I love you too, Nyx."

"Good, because I'm gonna fuck you like I hate you."

I line my dick up with her wet entrance and slam into her, making her walls clench, squeezing me tight.

"Oh, fuck." She moans.

Twisting my hand in her hair, I pull her head back and pound into her harder, getting beautiful noises from her. A day doesn't go by that she doesn't drive me wild. I don't know how I survived before her. I run my finger along the new tattoo on her ass cheek, three Halloween masks. Blue, green and red. Thank fuck a woman tattooed her because if another man had seen her ass, I would have lost it.

I pump harder just thinking about it. My fingers squeeze her hip, knowing tomorrow she'll have a bruise from my fingers.

"I need you screaming, baby." Moving my hand from her hair to her neck, her pussy squeezes me in response. "You like that, don't you?"

"Yeah, I love it when you choke me." She arched to meet my next thrust.

"Fucking." *Thrust.* "Perfect." *Thrust.* My fingers squeeze her neck tighter. "Fuck, baby. Your pussy is going to make me come."

Moving my hand from her throat to her clit, I rub fast, making her leg shake.

"That's it, baby, come around my dick. Let everyone know who owns it."

"Nyx, oh shiiit." She clamps around me hard, squirting as she comes.

I can't hold it in any longer. I spill deep inside her with a groan. I lay a gentle kiss on her neck before standing her up. Her legs shake, and she laughs.

"I think it's from digging the graves." She presses her lips to mine in a quick kiss.

"Haha, you're a funny one." I capture her mouth in a slow, saturated kiss. I begin to pull away when she locks her arms around my neck.

"Will you please talk to Cole? I don't like when you two fight. The tension is beginning to affect everyone in the house."

Her violet eyes plead with mine.

"I'll try, but Cole is pigheaded and always has been." You can't get a word in edge-wise with him. It's his way or the highway. Hence, why we're all still in the club.

She presses her lips to mine. "You can do it. Don't let him run all over you. You."—she pokes me in the chest.—"are not a doormat."

Where was she when I was growing up with my father? "Thanks, baby. Now, can we finish your work and worry less about me?"

"No. You can go. I can manage. Besides, I know how much you hate looking into the graves."

I rest my head on her forehead. "Thank fuck. It gives me bad mojo."

"Pussy." She laughs. "I'll see you in the morning."

"Please be safe." I run my hand through her hair before pulling her in for a hug. "Because I will kill anyone if they touch you again." I still regret not placing a bullet in her brother's fuckin' head that day on the street. I have nightmares of him coming back for her.

I wait until she reaches her next grave before I pull out. I figured I would take her advice and talk to Cole—what more damage could it possibly do to our relationship. Talking to him needs to be done in a certain way. Charging in like a wild boar will only end in another throwing match, which doesn't sound like a bad idea.

When I get home, I storm into the kitchen, where I hear Cole's voice. I don't bother saying hello, snapping my fingers and gaining Cole and Dorian's attention.

"You, asshole, to the basement. I'm settling some shit with you tonight."

He gives me a smirk. "Where the fuck were you?"

I can't help myself, I smirk back. "Banging your girlfriend, move it now."

Dorian snorts from his seat at the table. "I'm sure you were better than her other boyfriend?"

"Fuck you, asshole," Cole snaps. He brushes past me on his way to the basement.

"How is she?" Dorian asks.

I shake my head. "Tired of all our bullshit. I told her I would talk it out with dipshit but devised a better plan."

"Mmm, that explains it. I'll see you down there, eventually."

I race upstairs, finding my athletic shorts and changing into them. I find Cole warming up on the mats when I enter the basement. He's already panting—the disadvantage might just be mine.

"Get your ass in here, and you can tell me about Wednesday."

I finish wrapping my hands, shooting Cole a wide grin. Oh, I'll tell him about Cat, all right.

"Her pussy was begging for my dick, but that mouth." I lick my lips. "She had a few things to say about you."

I duck, missing his fist—always fighting with anger. "She told me to talk to you but figured this would be the best way."

He laughs. "She's smart." He's fast sweeping my feet from underneath me. I land on the mat with a thump.

"Fuck you, prick." I kick his shin, causing his balance to wobble. Jumping up, I punch his stomach hard. "I'm not taking your shit any longer, Cole."

"Is that so," he wheezes. A strand of black hair dangles on his wet forehead.

Adrenaline pulsed throughout my body. "Yeah, so next time a life-changing event happens, maybe let everyone have a say. You aren't my parent." My fist connects with his nose.

He wipes away the blood, laughing. If looks could kill, I'm sure my body would be a puddle of blood and a pile of bones. He takes a step forward, but thankfully, Dorian steps in the way.

"That's enough!" he yells, "Take your aggression out on the one that actually caused this."

"I'm so tired of this shit. I'm only trying to help." Cole rips his wraps off.

I grab a towel for his bleeding nose. "I get that, but Henry isn't listening, so it's useless." Handing it to him, he blots the blood.

"You two need to stop before you tear each other apart. Yelling and beating clearly aren't working. You need to beat Henry at his own game."

I flex my sore fingers. "What we need to do is get rid of Coleman."

That fuckin' mayor is no good for this town. Everyone needs to see what a douche he is. Exposing him is what we need to do before elections happen.

9

COLE

Nyx is right. The fighting needs to end. We're doing nothing but being complete assholes to each other when the enemy is out there causing a shit storm to our town. I dread coming to the compound for jobs now, knowing that Henry and Conrad are all about raving about the mayor and purge night coming up. Still not sure how it's our job to protect his ass.

I say let someone shoot the fucker.

That's actually not a bad idea. We could make it look like an accident. No one would suspect it if one of us went missing on patrol and shot him. We could act like the suspect outran us. *Oh, dang it*.

My phone goes off, and I roll over in bed to answer it.

"Yeah?"

"Good morning to you, too."

Henry, what a fuckin' lovely way to wake up.

"I have a job for you and the boys. Come down in half an hour, and I'll give you the details. Don't be late." He hangs up without waiting for me to reply.

I throw my phone somewhere on the bed; this is what I hate. The always-on-demand calls.

"You good?"

The one person I didn't think would stick by my side stands in the doorway, her dark hair piled high on her head with pieces framing her face, dark shadows smeared under her eyes. She looks irresistible wearing black booty shorts and a tank top.

I sit up in bed, patting the spot next to me. Henry can suck my dick for all I care. She comes first. "How was your night?" I placed a kiss on her forehead when she curled into my side.

"I'm so tired. I haven't been home long. The others are still sleeping."

Her body sinks into the feel of my arms wrapping around her. I don't want to leave. Panic furls deep in my chest at the thought of Halloween approaching.

"What about school? Are you headed in today?"

She nuzzles her head deeper into my neck. "I don't have class until later. Thankfully, it's my art class," she whispers quietly.

Her breathing evens out, and as much as I hate leaving her, I gently roll out of bed. "Love you with everything." I cover her with the blanket before heading to the bathroom.

Today will be stressful, and knowing Henry, it has to do with watching over the mayor. Here goes nothing. I'm sure the guys are gonna love this just as much as me.

∴⊥⋔⋔⊥⋔⋔⊥⋔⋔⋔∴⋔

The compound is busy when we all pull up. I think everyone is here, so this meeting is the top priority.

Freddy greets us when we step inside.

"You're late. He's going to lose his shit on you three."

"I had more important things to handle this morning."

Freddy grins. "How is our girl?"

"Working her ass to the grave, but she won't quit," Dorian scoffed.

Catalina and Freddy are two peas in a pod. You cannot separate them on Sundays when we get together. They became fast friends, and I love that.

"I'll have a chat with her on Sunday. For now, get your asses in there before Henry loses it." He nods to the hall. "He's in a mood, by the way."

"Perfect," Nyx mutters as he walks away.

I'm dreading this already. The second we walk in, the bitching will start. Henry will call Dorian a boy, and I'm not sure I'll be able to hold him back. It's the same old story.

Noise fills the hallway as we make our way to the meeting. The room falls silent when we walk in; scanning the room, my eyes land on Conrad, who grins at me. He has a punchable face.

"About time, boys. Only about," Henry looks at his watch, "fifteen minutes late. Sit down so we can finally start."

Dorian growls as he pulls his chair out. Spinning the chair backwards, he straddles it, crossing his arms on top of the back, narrowing his eyes at Henry.

Royce shakes his head, even though he knows this is bullshit. I might be able to persuade him to come with us when we leave. Henry starts talking, but I tune him out. My thoughts wander back to Cat. She looked beyond exhausted this morning. I feel most of it wasn't from work; it's from the added stress from all of our bullshit.

I'm trying not to bring it home, but like everything I touch, I ruin it. If only I wasn't always trying to out-think how my father raised me before child services stepped in. If only I was strong enough to remove those nasty memories.

Growing up in Southside, you always needed to think fast. If you weren't ahead in the races, you weren't eating that night. That's why I push the guys so much. I don't want them to end up in the gutter like I was. It took me years to get away from that side of town. Southside is rough; drugs are popular no matter who you are. Every other house would be a dealer or operation.

"Did you hear what I said, Cole?"

I blinked a few times, clearing my mind. "Yeah, I'm listening."

"So, you are good with driving Coleman around?"

The fuck did I miss? Why the hell would anyone wanna drive his ass around? Let alone me.

"That would be a fuck no."

Conrad shifts in his seat, and Royce straightens up. But Dorian and Nyx don't move a muscle. Oh, but Henry, his lip twitches just the slightest, and that left eye spazzes faster than a dog with the zoomies. I have to bite my lip so I don't laugh.

Henry stands, pushing his chair out with force. "You listen to me, you little shit. I'm the boss of this club, and what I say goes. You will do your job, or you'll suffer. Do you understand?"

I roll my eyes. "How the fuck will I suffer?"

He grins. "I would hate for anything to happen to that beautiful girl of yours."

I'm out of my seat along with Dorian and Nyx. "If you think about touching Catalina, I won't think twice about lighting your body on fire while you're still breathing."

"Then I suggest you do as I say." He leans further on the table, waiting for me to make a move.

Fuck! Fear and anger burn in my stomach. There's no way I'm letting him, or even Conrad, come anywhere near Cat. If I turn him down, he'll go after her. No matter how I play this, I have no choice but to do what Henry wants. He knew exactly what he was doing when he chose me.

"That's what I thought. You start tomorrow. Don't get Coleman killed." His eyes challenged mine.

"Don't ask for another fuckin' favour from me," I spat out. Dorian places his hand on my shoulder, giving it a squeeze.

"He understands. Nyx and I will be there to make sure he doesn't fuck it up." He tosses me a side-eye.

"What he said," I spoke lowly. Feeling defeated, what else am I supposed to do?

Conrad smirks. "I'll send over his itinerary and what he expects of you."

He gets what he gets. I'm not a fuckin' chauffeur. Maybe we'll get lost in Southside for fun.

I brush past Freddy without a second glance; I need out of the building—I can't think. The afternoon sun blinds me when I push open the door. I don't stop until I reach the firepit. Kicking the chairs over, I scream into the open air.

"We're fuckin' screwed. How are we going to protect Catalina and be with Coleman?" I turn to the guys, and they look just as scared as I am.

Nyx grabs me by the shoulder, pressing his forehead to mine. "We'll figure it out. Besides, Dorian and I can be with Cat when you are with Coleman. She never has to be alone."

"That's not the point."

"It is the point. Henry is only trying to mess with you. We won't let him get away with it." Dorian walks over, standing next to Nyx, placing his hand on my other shoulder. "We can do this together. We're family."

Closing my eyes, I take a deep inhale. I don't under-stand how they are so calm. They should be freaking out like I am. I need to see Cat now. My heart races with the thought of someone getting close to her again; for all I know, somebody could be watching her, waiting for the perfect time to strike.

Shaking off their hold. "I need to go, you guys can do what you need, but I have to go." I don't wait around for an answer. Moving quickly, I hop on my bike and peel out of the compound without a second glance. I'm losing faith in this club daily, and Nyx is right about one thing—leaving.

The ride to the University feels like ages before finally parking. The rev of two engines pulling alongside me doesn't surprise me either. I knew they would follow. Without a word, I storm off to the art building. That's what Cat said earlier; I hope that's where she still is.

"Why don't you call her?" Nyx says after storming into the building.

I didn't realize how big the art building was. Why are there so many different classes in painting on a canvas? Students give us a wide berth once they see the patch on our cuts, or it could be the look on my face that says. *Get in my way, and I'll fuck you up.* The Soul Stealers are now well known around town that we don't have to say anything for people to understand what we can do to them; it also doesn't help with that small *enforcer* patch on the chest. That usually makes people shut up.

"Because then she'll be freaked out, I'm only here because my mind is freaking out, and I need to calm it down," I tell him.

I continue to peek into each class, looking for her. After a few nasty glares from the teachers, I dig into my pocket. Contemplating about that phone call to her. She has to be okay. With all these people around, how can anyone find her? We can't even see her.

How do we still not know where her class is after all these months? I never thought to ask, honestly. After leaving this place, I was done. She had Nyx.

"You ass, don't you know where her class is?" I address Nyx.

"No, not this year. Last year, she was down a different hall."

Dorian rolls his eyes and takes his phone out of his pocket. "Bunch of pussies." He hits a button and places his phone to his ear. His grin says it all. "Hey darling, where are you?" He nods. "Okay, stay there, be there shortly. Love you." He slowly places his phone back into his pocket and then looks at Nyx and me.

"Well?" I throw my arms up.

"Room 3458. Wasn't so hard, now was it." He punches my arm when he walks by.

For him, maybe I would've sounded like a mess, and she would've known something was up. I'm the asshole, not the worried wart. I can't do this again. We need a normal life for once. We walk around until we find her classroom.

Walking in, I wouldn't call it a classroom; it's a fuckin' studio. Bookshelves line the back wall with paint, paint-brushes and other necessary painting supplies. Another wall is filled with canvases of various sizes. I've never seen such a thing unless I took Cat to an art supply store.

My eyes land on her, and my chest finally feels relief. She sits in front of her canvas with a paint streak on her cheek, her black hair tied into a messy bun without a care in the world.

She scans the room, watching all three of us. "What's going on? You guys never come see me." She places her paintbrush in the water, swivelling on her stool to face us. "Don't bullshit me. What happened today, Cole?"

How can I tell her anything without throwing a fist through the wall? All I want is to bring her an ounce of happiness. I feel like every day, I'm failing. Why can't I protect her the way I see in my mind? It's like Henry knows what I want and sends a fuckin' grenade and explodes it without a second thought.

"Cole," her voice goes low. "Tell me now."

My shoulders slump. "Catalina, I need you to stay close to Nyx or Dorian from now on. Things have changed in the club, and I don't think you're safe anymore."

"Why?"

"Things happened. I'm not going into detail. Once you are done here, please come home." I get closer to her, inhaling her apple and honey scent. I dropped a kiss on her forehead. "Please, Cat. I won't be able to survive if anything happens again," I whisper against her skin.

She thinks about it for a while. "I promise."

I grip her chin, tipping her head back. "You best keep that fuckin' promise, Wednesday."

She laughs. "Or what?"

Dorian moves behind her. "Or you'll be punished," he whispers in her ear.

A small smile moves across her lips.

"You wanna be punished, baby?" Nyx strokes his finger down her cheek.

I love watching her get all turned on by all three of us.

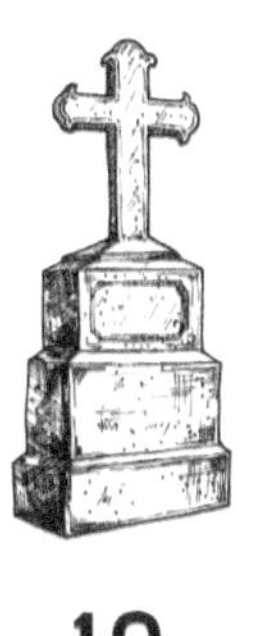

10

DORIAN

Deep down, I know what Cole is going through. We all want Catalina safe, but I have a feeling it's going to be a challenge. Watching her sit here with all three of us as we surround her is how I want her daily. She licks her lips, and I know exactly what she wants. Moving my hands down her waist, dipping into the waistband of her leggings. The heat from her pussy warms my hand; I don't need to guess how wet she is.

"Half pint, do you need to be punished?" I run my finger around her clit, getting the sweetest moan from her.

"Maybe I do." She grabs my wrist, pinning it to her body. "But unfortunately for you, the next class will be here shortly."

I rub my finger faster; a punishment is what she'll get even if I have a limited time. Her nails dig into my skin the closer she gets to finishing. Cole moves to her side, sliding his hand under her shirt and cupping her breast.

"We need you to come fast for us, little one. Or you won't come at all until you get home."

Her head falls back, and Nyx takes the opportunity to kiss along her neck. Dipping my finger further down, I sink into her wet core, not stopping until I hit her g-spot.

"Fuck, baby. Seeing you like this makes me want to come in my pants like a teenage boy." Nyx continues to kiss along her jaw.

She laughs, but it becomes a moan when I stroke her g-spot faster.

"Fuck, Dorian. Don't stop, please," she begs.

"I love it when you beg me. How much do you want this?"

Cole lifts her shirt, exposing her breasts. Pinching her taught nipple, she squeezes around my finger.

"I want it so bad, please. I need to come more than anything."

Nyx hums. "Do you. Are you going to listen to us?"

"Yes."

"Are you going to do everything we say?" Cole asks. "Without putting up a fight?"

She's silent. I withdraw my finger.

"Yes!" she screams. "Please make me come."

"Such a good girl, aren't you?" I push two fingers in, pumping fast until my fingers are drenched. She comes fast, slamming her eyes shut; she moans our names. I'll never get tired of hearing her coming for us.

Cole fixes her shirt, trying to score those brownie points. When she looks at me, I lick my fingers clean.

"Thanks for the treat, darling. I'll give you something to lick off when you get home."

She smirks. "You wish, bucko, but work calls again tonight."

Cole glares at her. "You go with one of them or no work at all. I told you they stick with you no matter what."

She jumps off the stool, getting in his face. "I'm not an idiot, Cole. But I won't suck a dick when I'm trying to meet a quota. I already got my ass chewed out from the other day when Nyx rammed me in the cemetery. I have a job to do besides be a little fuck toy for you three."

I'm speechless. Is that what she thinks? Nyx takes a step back, looking at the floor.

"You could've said no," he mutters.

"You guys don't even take me on dates. What do you expect me to think.?"

My shoulders drop; I don't have an excuse.

Maybe one. We're shitty boyfriends.

Cole backs away, adding more distance. That worries me; Cole doesn't have to say words to say what he means. He's telling her what she's telling all of us.

"If you want out, there's the door, Catalina. No one is stopping you. You're the one that didn't want dates!"

She crosses her arms. "That's beside the point. And this is my fuckin' school. You can leave. You don't belong here." Her lips curl with disgust. I slowly move in, wrapping my arm around her shoulders.

"Cat, maybe we should talk about this when we all get home." I practically pleaded with her. She shrugs my arm off before storming to the door.

"Get out." Swinging the door open, she waits. "I mean it. You can't keep controlling me. This isn't how a relationship works. I'll be home after school."

Cole leaves first, not looking at her when he walks past her. She closes her eyes. When Nyx walks up to her, he pulls her into a hug. Her arms never leave her side. My heart breaks—the distance she's placing between us is slowly growing. I'm not sure what could be done to bring her back after this. I'm afraid she'll never forgive us.

Nyx whispers in her ear, but she never responds or blinks. Standing like a statue, I move closer, cupping her cheeks. I tilt her head back, staring into her violet eyes.

"Listen to me, Catalina. If I only wanted a fuck toy, I would've found anyone around this shitty ass town to fill that position. I wanted somebody to spend the rest of my life with, someone to have babies with. We would grow old and chase our dreams together. I chose you to be that somebody." Tears fill her eyes. "Why on earth do you think we act the way we do? We all love you and would do anything for you. But if you need time to find yourself, please take it. Don't think for a minute we won't be in the shadows, not watching over you." I breathe her in when I place my last kiss on her forehead. I leave her alone in that classroom with nothing but my heart and a fuckin' prayer that she'll return to us.

Cole and Nyx leave me alone while I wait for Cat to finish her classes. I wasn't kidding when I told her we would be watching from a distance. With the way Henry was talking, I don't trust that asshole. The way he's acting with this new purge has my hair standing on edge. I'm not sure what he gets out of it for opening it up to surrounding towns. All I can see is a mess coming from it, and I'm tired of cleaning up his and Coleman's shit.

A wave of raven hair flutters in the wind, and I instantly know my half-pint is finished for the day. I straighten up on my bike, waiting for her to get into her Beetle. She looks around, trying to find one of us, but she won't see me. I hid too well. Shaking her head, she opens her car door, tossing her bag in. With a defeated look, she climbs in. The second she leaves, I start my bike. Cole and Nyx are staying away from the house tonight; if she chooses to move out, there's nothing we can do.

On the ride to the house, my nerves are on fire. I'm not sure if my body is vibrating from them or from my bike. When she parks in the driveway, I stay on the street. Shutting my bike off, I remain seated until her door opens.

"Dorian, I don't need a chaperone," she calls from the edge of her car.

"I also told you someone would be watching you. Cole even said you wouldn't be alone. You need to start listening." I shrug, not giving a shit.

"I won't be long," she says as she enters the house.

I pull my phone out of my pocket. It's best to rip the bandage off fast, especially with Cole.

Me: She's leaving.

Cole: Jesus fucking Christ.

Nyx: For how long?

Me: I'm not sure. She didn't say much.

Cole: I knew this would happen.

Nyx: Maybe it's for the best. We have too much shit going on.

Nyx isn't wrong. But is she really safer out there without us? Where the hell is she going to stay? She gave up her apartment when she moved in with us. It's not like she has any friends she can crash with or family.

She exits the house carrying a hockey bag. That seals the deal. She's moving out. I hop off my bike, rushing to help.

She holds her hand up. "Don't. I got this."

"Where are you staying?"

"I called Riley. He said I could crash at his place."

Right. I guess she does have a friend, after all. Nodding, I let her finish hauling her bags to the car before I march over and grab her wrist.

"We aren't giving up on you. I hope you know this."

She takes a deep breath, closes her eyes, and slowly exhales. "I know, Dorian. But I think we all rushed into everything after what happened last year. Give me a week to think things through, please."

"A week, and then we're coming for you." I step back, giving her the space she needs.

"Thank you. I do love you. I hope you know that."

I give a small smile before I walk back to my bike. A week, that's all I'm promising, nothing more and nothing less. It'll be torture, but it could be worse. She could be gone forever.

Me: She's headed to Riley's.

Nyx: I'll follow her.

I get three dots from Cole, but he never replies.

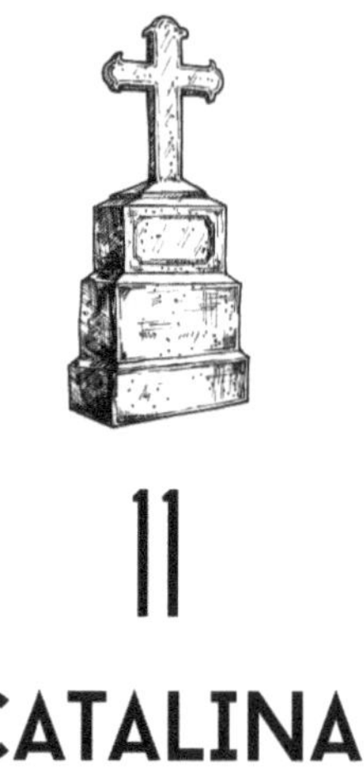

11

CATALINA

I probably flew off the handle, but I feel like I'm never heard when they are around. As I pull into Riley's driveway, he's at the doorway, holding a mug and chocolate.

"What's this?" I ask when I get out of Johnny.

"I don't know what girls do after a breakup." He blushes.

Did I break up with the guys, though? I'm giving them a week to see if they can straighten up—I'm not even sure at this point. Maybe I'm doing them a favour and being less of a burden when they are stressing about the club and Halloween.

I grab the mug of hot chocolate from Riley and follow him inside. "Thanks again for letting me stay here. I didn't have anyone else to call."

He waves me off. "Don't worry about it. I'm hardly home, anyway."

His house is on the smaller side, roomy enough for two. You can also tell a bachelor has been shacking up in here. The living room is filled with his medical books, a small couch and a desk. He leads me into his kitchen and I hold back a laugh. Paper plates overfill his garbage.

"I don't do dishes. I barely cook, so hopefully, you can feed yourself."

"Don't worry. Dorian has taught me a few things." Just mentioning his name sends a ping to my chest. Riley stares at me for a second before he continues his tour. We walk down the hallway, and he points to the only bathroom.

"Sorry, we'll have to share."

"That's fine. I hope you don't mind girly shit lying around." I laugh when I look inside the bathroom. The countertop is covered with his shaving products, deodorant and absolutely no room for my things.

"Um, if you can find room."

I pat him on the shoulder. "It's only for a week. I'm not messy, don't worry."

He tilts his head. "Your room is this way. I keep it clean for when my mom comes down."

I poke my head in. His mom has to be the one who cleans it. The bed is made like a mom would do it. Or I would assume that's how a mom would make it. I was constantly yelled at if I didn't make mine a certain way, and if that didn't work, her son would come in. Shivers roll down my back with the thought of them.

Riley touches my shoulder. "You, okay?"

"Yep. I'll go grab my bags. I still have to work tonight." I try to cover my yawn.

"I'll help. My mom would tan my hide if she found out otherwise."

My plan is to dig until I forget. Nothing can sidetrack me tonight; a fuckin' earthquake could happen, and I still wouldn't stop. I know I can't change the guys, and never in my life would that go through my mind. But just for once, can't I be treated like a girlfriend? Maybe I'm asking for too much, and dating three guys simultaneously might be too much. Did they even want that in the first place? I'm thinking too hard, I'm getting a headache.

One Week Later

I'll be the first to admit living with another guy is hell.

"Jesus H Christ." I kick Riley's dirty boxers out of the way for the tenth time this week. "And you wonder why you're single still." All I want is a shower. Working and living with someone are entirely different points of view. I like the working Riley better; he's cleaner.

My phone dings from my bedroom. It could be Dr. Deadbodies or one of the guys. I'm in no hurry to talk to any of them, to be honest. My art project is number one and needs all of my attention. I have two months left of school, and I'm finished for good. Everyone can wait until this afternoon for any answers from me. Besides, Davis knows where I'll be if he needs me.

On my way to the university, I stop at a small café for something hot to drink; when I walk past the window, a flyer has me stopping.

ANNUAL PURGE NIGHT FOR THE TOWN OF EASTWOOD HAS RETURNED!

HAPPENING THIS HALLOWEEN, BIGGER AND BETTER THAN BEFORE.

RULES FOR HALLOWEEN NIGHT STARTING AT 7 PM.

1. ALL ACTIVITIES END AT 7 AM

2. IF YOU ARE CAUGHT GOOD LUCK

3. ANYTHING GOES ON THIS NIGHT

4. TAKE NO PITY FOR THOSE THAT DON'T CELEBRATE

DON'T FORGET TO VOTE FOR MAYOR COLEMAN.

"What the fuck?" I can't believe people are hanging this shit up. How can the mayor get away with this still? This town is fucking crazy that's what it is. Do I still want my drink from this business? Do these people even know what goes on after dark? I certainly do. Look where that got me. I turn around and head back to Johnny, my mood turning sour. Thank God I can splatter some paint on my canvas today.

The only thing about that flyer that concerns me is the *anything goes*. What exactly does that mean? Before, it was to crave Coleman's sexual fantasies. Does he have another fantasy in mind this year? Purges usually mean one thing. To cleanse. What the fuck is he cleansing? He can't cleanse his dick every year.

I would like to cleanse him off this earth if possible. That's not a bad idea, actually. I have a few empty graves that need to be filled in.

I park my car with more attitude than needed; that sour mood won't be gone for hours at this rate. I wonder which guy tailed me today; it wouldn't be Cole, that's for sure. He has a way of making his presence known.

My art professor is a pain in the asshole this semester. I've been trying to get this piece done all week, but no matter what I do, it keeps turning out like absolute garbage. The colours keep muddling together, and I can't get the shading right. I'm tempted to trash it and start over, but with my luck, the clock will run out on me again. This piece counts for more than half my grade.

I should've done the stupid sculptor like I was planning on.

"Cat, you could combine the two."

My nosey neighbour points out. She's a slacker, so I wouldn't be taking her advice, but this time, she's kinda right. It would be wise. Cover up the shit mess with a blob of crap.

"Thanks," I mutter.

After painting my canvas black, I started sculpting something even darker, from which my childhood was created.

"You worthless child. You can't do anything right even after explaining it to you repeatedly." My mother snubs her nose at me.

"I'm trying, I swear."

"You're embarrassing me. Do you think your brothers would do this?"

I don't answer; most of her questions are traps. The teacher watches us from her desk, never coming to rescue me. No matter how much I try to plead for it. No one ever does. I'm used to saving myself for so long that relying on someone else only ends in disappointment.

"Mrs. Wilson, is there anything you want to discuss before the next parent comes in?"

Mother scoffs in disgust at me before turning her attention to the teacher. "Is she always this slow in class?"

"I'm sorry?"

"Her grades. They could be better. Her brothers never had such shit grades before."

My teacher stands there shocked. "I can assure you that Catalina is a brilliant student, Mrs. Wilson—"

"I find that shocking. Her head is stuck in the clouds. Her art isn't important and won't get Catalina anywhere in life. Focus her studies somewhere else."

My mother digs her claws into my arms, dragging me out of the classroom.

That was the day that I said fuck you and focused on my art. I stare at my sculptor on my table, and my hands shake. Even after all this time, I can still picture her hands and those long fingernails. I swear my arm throbs in pain at the memory of them digging into my skin.

My mind has to be tired if it's bringing up that memory. I was doing good at blocking her. It has to be the stress from the past week. I quickly pack up; my mind can't be anywhere near this mess at the moment. When I reach my car, Nyx is waiting for me.

"Baby." Nyx pushes off my car—regret shining in his brown eyes. "Please come home." Meeting me halfway, he reaches for my hand. I swing it out of the way at the last second.

"I'm not sure I'm ready for that yet, Nyx. I have some more thinking to do."

His hand curls into a fist. "But you said a week."

"I know what I said. It's just." Pinching the bridge of my nose.

"You need more time, don't you?" His warm hand caresses mine.

How can I tell him I'm unsure about this relationship without sounding like a bitch?

"Hey, listen. We're here for you, no matter your decision, but you need to talk to us. Whatever you need, we all want to give it to you. Let me know when you want to talk." He drew me in, and I breathed his spice and citrus smell. I won't lie; I've missed how he can calm me down, and after today I needed this.

I can't get caught up in him. It's dangerous, and I need to keep an open mind. I step back, creating distance.

"Can I call you when I'm ready to talk?"

"Sure. You working tonight?"

I walk to my car. "Don't act like you don't know my schedule," I call over my shoulder.

"I know everything about you. You're my girlfriend."

"Prove it." I don't bother turning around.

"You like to keep everyone at a distance because you're afraid of being hurt. You hang around the dead because they keep your secrets. Catalina, you might think we don't pay attention, but you can't hide from us. We all want to be your boyfriends if that's what has you worried; we love sharing you."

Tears sting my eyes. It's not fair that he knew exactly what was bothering me. Here I thought I was a closed book. Yet he ripped me open and tore each page out one by one. It shouldn't surprise me. He's the one who knows me the most out of all three of them.

"I'll see you later, Nyx."

I don't have anything else to say. What can I say that he hasn't already?

12

NYX

The week without Catalina felt like the Dark Ages. And now watching her leave isn't helping me either. Those lonely feelings are creeping in again, and I'm not sure if I'll survive them this time around. When this happened last time, I knew deep down we would get her back, but now, I have doubts. Something is eating at her, and she won't open up.

I follow her until she reaches Riley's, then take off to the house. There are a few things I need to discuss with the guys. Number one is how she doesn't feel confident in this relationship. I know for a fact she doesn't believe we all want her equally.

From someone who wasn't wanted, I know what that feels like; I would give her anything in this world and the one after if that's what she wants. But I can't do this alone. I want her with all of them, or it won't feel the same.

Storming through the door, voices come from the kitchen. It hasn't been quiet around here for days. I interrupt Cole and Dorian mid-fight.

"I talked to her today."

They both freeze. Cole stares at me. His blue eyes widen in shock.

"What did she say?"

Dorian runs his hand through his blond hair, tugging at the ends. "Please tell me she's coming home."

Cringing, I slowly shake my head.

"Fuck!" Cole roars, punching the countertop.

The trim busts off, landing on the floor. "Fuck this. She's coming home, whether she likes it or not. She's acting like a child."

"Cole, haven't you figured it out by now? She wants to be heard in this relationship, and you acting like a fuckin' idiot isn't helping," Dorian pointed out.

"To be honest, I think she feels like we never wanted to share her," I add.

"That's stupid," Cole and Dorian say.

I shrug. "It's the impression I got from her earlier. She's working tonight if somebody wants to take the night shift."

"I have to drive dickhead around as per my orders."

"Just finish Coleman off and be done with his ass. Have you seen the flyers around town?" Dorian asks.

I pull one out of my back pocket, unfold it, and toss it on the counter. "This shit. I found it at the café this morning.

Cat was reading it. I can't believe he talked all these people into hanging this shit around town. I wonder how many people are believing this shit."

"My issue is how many towns are going to take part in it." Cole reads the flyer, chewing his lip. "What happens when more people flock into town, and we aren't able to keep it safe like before."

"Then we do what we have to by any means." I shrug. "Besides, it's not like the cops are going to do anything."

Only two towns surround Eastwood, but how far can word spread that purge night is a free-for-all. This year is going to be bigger than anyone has expected in the past. With more outsiders, it's going to cause more issues; the one I'm afraid of is murder.

Catalina cannot go outside.

"We have one more week until Halloween. We should figure out what to do in the meantime with Catalina. Especially if she doesn't come home."

Cole glares at Dorian. "She's coming home. If she wants boyfriends, then that's what she'll fuckin' get." He marches out of the kitchen, and the front door slams shut.

"He's taking it hard but still won't talk about it," Dorian admits.

"Is that what you two were arguing about?"

Dorian walks to the fridge, opening it to grab a beer. He offers me one, and we sit silently for a while, sipping our beers. I wait until Dorian starts; whatever they were fighting about must've been serious if he hasn't spilled the beans already.

"Cole thinks we should take Coleman out."

"Out? As in," I run my finger along my neck.

Dorian nods. "Yeah, he figures since he drives him around, he'll have access to him on Halloween. The only issue I have is who's going to keep the town on track and Cat."

Where is the safest place for her? I can't even say the cemetery since that's where we found her. But we also knew about her last year. We had her in our sights for a long time. That's how we knew she was the one.

"What if she stayed with Riley for the night?"

"Is he trustworthy? Do we know he doesn't take part in the purge?"

I take another swig, that I'm not sure of.

Dorian finishes his drink. "Don't get me wrong, he seems like a good enough guy, and he's letting her stay with him, but I'm not sure."

"Cole will flip his lid if we bring it up. What if we kept her at the school? She still has access to the medical department. We drop her off. Her car won't be near the school that way. No one would know she's there."

"Only one problem." He looks at me, rubbing his chin. "Catalina."

She'll put up a fight worse than Cole will. But, like it or not, it's for her own protection. Even if I have to tie her down. Her ass is not going outside.

"I'll watch her tonight. Do you know which cemetery she's at?"

"She's in Eaglewood. I hate that cemetery. The fact that she's out of town, anything can happen there."

I'm still amazed that even after all this time, she has bodies to dig up. How doesn't this school have funding for cadavers? How does this town have that many people dying? Something is happening here, that's for sure; it's got to be coming from Southside.

"When you go with her tonight, can you look for gang symbols on the bodies?"

"You have a suspicion about something?"

I tap my head. "Something like that."

That night, when Dorian comes home, he looks exhausted. I hoped he would walk through the door with our beautiful, gothic, loving girl. But she's nowhere in sight. My heart bottoms out when I realize she was telling me the truth earlier today. She isn't ready to come home yet.

"How did it go?" AKA any gang members in the dirt.

He blows a heavy breath out. "It went."

I motioned my hands for him to continue.

"Where's Cole at?" He walks past me into the kitchen. I follow behind, noticing how tense he is.

Whatever happened tonight can't be good. "He's downstairs. I'll grab him."

Opening the basement door, I call down for Cole; all that can be heard is his music being blasted. Flicking the light switch to grab his attention, he cuts his music off.

"Yeah, what?" he growls.

"Dorian has something he wants to talk to us about."

His weights slam down, and he appears at the bottom of the stairs, sweat pouring off his face. "This better be worth it."

I wait until he's closer. "Well, he didn't look happy if that makes you feel better."

He shoots me a glare. "Not really, Nyx."

When we enter the kitchen, Dorian is drinking whiskey. He slides the bottle toward us. "Here. You'll need this."

I pour two fingers' worth into my glass before sliding it to Cole. He holds the bottle; we rarely drink a lot because it reminds him of his father. Eventually, he pours some into his glass.

"Spill it, Dorian, what happened tonight." Cole doesn't even break eye contact as he slams his drink back.

"Nyx wanted me to check the bodies that half pint was digging up for markings." He takes a sip of his whiskey. "I don't think she ever paid attention to any of the bodies she dug up before. I even asked, and she just called them John or Jane Does. She never wants to think about what she's doing in case family members come looking around."

Okay, so everything sounds completely normal so far.

"So, why do you look like this then?"

"Because you asked me to check for gang markings, asshole, and I found them."

"Shit," Cole mumbles.

"On all the bodies she dug up?" I asked.

Dorian leans his forearms on the counter. "She dug up three bodies tonight, two females and one male. Both females belonged to the Death Eaters. Cat had no idea what their markings looked like. The male was elderly."

"And Davis goes through the paper to find these bodies? Cause I highly doubt the gang will place obituaries in the paper." Cole points out.

"Unless they know someone is digging up the bodies and know it's a way of disposing of their members without the cops snooping around."

"Henry is still watching the cemeteries the odd night, too. He wanted me to keep an eye on it the other night." I mentioned, displeasure clear as day. I hated doing that job. I had no choice because I was sure Conrad had men following me.

Little did he know, I ensured Catalina didn't work those days. The 'Can't see you' texts are code, and it's been working.

"Do you think Henry knows what the Death Eaters are doing?" I stare at Cole.

He scoffs, rolling his eyes. "I'm sure that's where Henry is burying his dead, too. Where else would everyone go?"

Jesus, this entire time, Catalina has been digging up our members and not knowing it. She's lucky that she hasn't been caught. I don't want to think what Henry would do to her if he did catch her. My stomach turns the more I think about it.

"Where is Cat now?"

"I helped her at the school, then escorted her to Riley's. She wouldn't give me an answer as to when she'll be home. I don't think she even knows. We didn't talk much about where we are headed, I followed her lead, and whatever she needed, that's what I did."

"Fuckin' pussy. She needs to be pushed in the right direction."

"No, Cole." I narrow my eyes at him. "That's what got us in a mess, to begin with. You and your bossy personality."

Cole shoves me. "I'm not bossy."

"You are bossy, you asshole." Catalina stood motionless at the entrance to the kitchen, staring at each of us.

"Wednesday." Cole steps closer. "You came home?"

She drops her bag. "I couldn't sleep, so I'm home."

Ten pounds of pressure fell from my chest. But I feel like she's about to drop another bomb on us.

13

COLE

When people say things are too good to be true, fuckin' believe them. Having Catalina at home is fantastic, but it's been two days, and she hasn't let any of us hold or kiss her. It's like living in the doghouse, and I'm trying to figure out what I did wrong.

All right, I know what I did wrong. I'm the worst boyfriend in the history of boyfriends, but she should know this. I'm not dating material; I have no account of a stable household. Give me an addicted father figure, and I can handle them; a shitty foster parent, no problem. But a girlfriend, I'm not sure what to do with them. I'm not a fancy date and flower-giving person.

I've tried googling ideas, but they all seemed so lame. Catalina isn't the type of person you take to the movies and dinner. I have a better idea, thankfully; I don't have to drive dickhead around tonight, and she doesn't have any jobs.

I hope she likes this surprise.

"Dorian, can you make something for Catalina and me?"

He looks up from his phone. "Why?"

I rub my face, trying to keep my cool. "Because asshole, I don't need to kill her with my cooking."

He goes back to scrolling on his phone. "Well, no shit. But the question remains. Why?"

I can see the wheels turning in his head; he'll make fun of me and probably tell me how lame it is. Everything else I thought of was stupid and wouldn't be fun.

"Do it for her then. It would be a lot for her to go on a date."

"I would've done it, anyway. I wanted to give you a hard time." He throws his phone on the couch and gets up.

I, on the other hand, step toward him. "You sonofabitch." Punching him in the arm. "Don't be a dick."

He hisses, rubbing his arm. "Fuck you. Learn how to cook. Or I'll only pack enough to feed Cat." He heads for the kitchen, then stops. "Are you serious about killing Coleman?"

"Like a fuckin' heart attack."

"I'll get everything figured out; I'll talk to Freddy, get the torture room all setup, and make sure no one is around the compound for us."

God, Halloween is going to be one long, bloody night. And I'm going to love every minute of it.

I'm loading up my saddle bag when Catalina pulls into the driveway. A fishnet-clad leg kicks the driver's door open when I look up. Her black mini skirt shows just the right amount of thigh that has too much blood rushing to my cock.

Her violet eyes lock onto mine when she notices me. How she ever thought we never wanted her blows my mind; I would fight for her until the end of time.

"Cole." She looks at my bike, then back to me. "Where are you going?"

"Go get pants on. I have somewhere that I wanna show you."

She hesitates for a second. Staring at me, then the house. I'm not sure what she's expecting. I get that we always do things as a group most of the time. Or that I never initiate stuff between us, but I'm trying to be a better boyfriend.

"Yeah, give me a minute. I'll be back."

I'm nervous and excited. I've never taken anyone to this place before. All I can do now is wait. When ten minutes pass, I panic. Is she even going to come out? Dorian and Nyx are inside; they wouldn't talk her out of coming, would they?

I'm having an internal battle with myself. I didn't hear anyone sneak up on me.

"Ready?"

She still takes my breath away, no matter how often I see her. She's ready to ride with her hair braided to the side, a long-sleeved shirt, and black skinny jeans. Since day one, I've been itching to take her out on my bike. I've just never had the time.

"I'm always ready for you, Wednesday." I strap her helmet on, brushing her cheek; she turns and waits. "You'll have to actually touch me on the ride."

Mounting my bike, I wait. Her legs press against mine, and it feels like heaven. This is where she belongs and nowhere else.

"Where are we going?" she asks after she wraps her arms around my waist.

"I want to show you something, so I figured I'd turn it into a date." I glance back to see her eyes widen.

"Oh. I would love that, Cole. Thank you."

Without a word, I start the bike and pull out of the driveway. I hope taking her back to Southside doesn't bring back horrible memories, but what I have to show her will hopefully make her understand me better.

Once you cross that line between town, it's a different ball game. I still can't believe I grew up here and that I didn't do worse shit with my life. The house that Cat was in when her asshole of a brother kidnapped her was burned down. Dorian couldn't stand the thought of having that place standing. I don't blame him. The way her brother did things still bothers me. Why stalk and kidnap her? The torture of her childhood wasn't enough, you had to continue even when she was happy. For what a couple of pennies, that's what bothers me. Why not just talk to her? She would've handed it over in a heartbeat.

Her grip tightens when we get further into Southside. I take her hand, placing it over my heart. It's steady, reminding her she's safe with me.

Turning down the street where my father tried to raise me, memories flood back.

"Hey, you little shit, hand me that bottle."

Dad's been on the liquor for three days, and I've been walking on eggshells. I've been doing everything possible not to be home, but the cops found me hiding behind the old junkyard and hauled me back. I hated those pricks. Why couldn't they haul my dad away? Things would be easier without him around.

"Here." I toss him his bottle of Jack. "Don't get too drunk. You have to work tomorrow."

His head snaps up fast. "The fuck you say to me?" Stumbling, he moves quickly. Grabbing me by my shirt, he gets into my face. His breath smells like stale beer. "You don't tell me what to do with my life, do you understand?"

"I can tell you what to do if I have to. You don't do anything around here anymore," I spit in his face.

Shoving me hard, I land on my ass. He stared down at me with his precious bottle in his hand. "You should've died alongside your mother. You don't deserve to be breathing."

I'm not sure if it was luck or not, but that asshole ended up being killed at work the next day. I think karma had a way of working its magic.

I park the bike across the street from the broken house. What once was a mint house is now painted in graffiti from the vandals having fun. Fuck, I hate this place with a passion. It's another place I would love to see burned.

With a deep breath, I turn to look at Catalina. "This is where I grew up for most of my life." She takes in the house and the neighbourhood, not that there's much to take in. Every other place doesn't look any better.

"It's fine. You can say it looks like shit. I won't lie. Growing up here was shit."

"What happened after here?"

"I moved to a foster home until I turned eighteen. It was somewhat better than living with him, but they still treat you like garbage. They only want you for the pay cheque."

She bites her lip, looking nervous. I have a feeling I already know the question that's coming. It's something I never talk about.

"And your mom? You never talk about her."

"That's because she's dead, Wednesday." Her hand grips my bicep. "Don't feel bad. She died when I was three. A car accident, I think. We did not talk about here a lot in that shithole. Only when he started drinking, he always said that I didn't deserve to be breathing either."

"Jesus, Cole. How could someone ever talk to their child that way?" I stare at her, and she nods. "Right, never mind. I get it."

"But I have something else to show you. Hold on."

Pulling away from the nightmare, I take her to a hidden spot no one can find. It's deep in Southside that Dorian, Nyx and I would hide out in when we were younger.

Taking an invisible roadway behind the junkyard, it's surprising that it hasn't been overgrown with weeds yet. The gravel pit is precisely the same; I'm not even sure they use this place anymore. Most of the gravel piles have grass growing out of them, and the equipment has rusted to shit from the rain. And the fire pit we used to use is still here.

It'll be a perfect spot for Cat to finally relax and forget about the week of hell we put her through.

Dorian's lunch, of course, is over extreme. I would've been okay with peanut butter and jam sandwiches, but whatever. Catalina is happy, and that's all that matters.

"Why take me out on a date after all this time?" she asks, taking a bite of her pasta salad.

I mix my salad around, flicking the onions out. "It shouldn't be surprising that I'm not boyfriend material, Cat. I don't know anything about this shit. All I know is not to beat you. I don't know anything else."

She moves closer, taking my hand. "Cole, I don't expect the moon from you. I knew from the start that you didn't want anything to do with me. It was no lie that you had a hard time with us. And don't believe for a second I think your bullying shit is why you found me that night. I know better."

I'll admit it was a lame excuse, but in my defence, it didn't look good that she was creeping around at night to see an older man from school. There was something different about her.

"I wanted you to be mine."

She laughs. "You had a weird way of showing it. Did you have to wait until purge night?"

"Yes, how else would we know you had some kinks to work out."

Straddling me, she brushes a piece of hair out of my face. "I love this date. I only have one question."

"Okay."

"You aren't expecting anything from this date, are you?"

Stroking her cheek, I work my way down her neck. She swallows hard the further I dip. "There's only one thing I want, Catalina." Lying her on the blanket, I push her top up, exposing her breasts. "I want you coming."

Taking a nipple in my mouth, I bite it before sucking on it. Her hips raise to meet with my growing cock, and fuck does that feel amazing, but this isn't about me—I need to give her what she wants. Popping her nipple from my mouth, I take the other one, and her sweet moans fill the air. A sound I'll never get tired of hearing. But I need them a touch louder.

Moving my hand lower, I unsnap her jeans. "Tell me, little one. What do you want?"

She shifts, getting even closer. "What sort of tricks do you have in your bags?"

I grin, always up for an adventure. I have just the thing. Working fast, I open my saddlebag to find what I need. It doesn't take me very long. Oh, I can't wait to play; it's been a while since she let me do whatever I wanted. She doesn't disappoint either when I reach her. Lying naked on the blanket with her legs spread wide, she's damn near dripping.

"Fuck me."

"Only if you want to."

I drop the rope and lube. It's been a while since I've tied her up, and I'm going to enjoy this.

"You remember your safe word?"

"Yes," she agrees. Getting on her knees for me. I run my hand along her collarbone, producing goosebumps.

"Perfect, little one." Grabbing the rope, we worked hard to overcome her fear of having her arms tied, and I couldn't be prouder of her. I tie her hands together in a cat claw. Once satisfied, I move her hand between her legs, lowering her head to the blanket. Wrapping the rope around her right ankle, I do the same to her left. I swirl the remaining rope until I finish it into a frog tie. Her ass is perfectly positioned in the air for my liking.

"Does this feel okay?"

"Um, yeah," she struggles to answer.

I tug the rope. "You sure? I can loosen or take them off."

"No, I love it. I want this."

Smacking her ass to be sure, her pussy becomes wetter. Spreading her cheeks apart, I run my finger around her asshole. "I'm fucking this ass until you come, do you understand?"

"Yes." She struggles against the rope.

Squirting some lube along her crack, I ease my finger in, working it back and forth. Pushing her ass toward me, I know what she wants. Ever since the first time she had anal, she's been hooked. Unbuckling my belt, I pull my throbbing cock out. Adding another finger, she looks gorgeous with the ropes tied around her body.

Smacking my cock on her ass several times, I line up against her tight hole. Gripping the rope, my piercing pressing tight against her opening as I push deep inside slowly, the squeeze she has on me makes me pause.

"God, you're so fucking tight, I can't handle it." I pull out until the tip is left in, slamming back in; she moans, gripping the rope beneath us.

Without remorse, I pound hard into her, and I swear stars shoot across my vision the longer I go. I know this is supposed to be about her, but I can't help but enjoy it too.

"I love it when you're rough with me. Sorry that I've been a bad girlfriend."

I find her wet entrance and shove two fingers deep inside. "You've been a fuckin' brat is what you've been."

"Ahh, fuck," she groans, pushing her ass back into me, taking me deeper.

Stroking her g-spot, she clamps down on my fingers and groans louder as she reaches her climax. I want to see her squirt before I finish in her ass. Moving my other hand, I rub her clit fast.

"I want you to be as loud as possible when you come." Not letting up, I move both hands faster until her body shakes. She's so close, but she won't give in. Jerking my hips forward, I give her everything I have. All the sensations all at once. My body is in hyper-drive as her body clings to me.

My climax is rearing to go; if she doesn't finish soon, I will. Moving my hand away from her clit, I pull her hips into me, fucking her fast and hard.

"Fucking, come. I want everything you have." Pressing my fingers harder on her g-spot, she finally let go, soaking the blanket beneath us. Fuckin' heaven. Getting into a low squat and grabbing her shoulders, I can fuck her how I want.

"Cole, come in my mouth. I want to taste you."

"Anything for you, little one," I groan.

I don't stop fucking her until I'm about to explode. It feels too good to stop. Pulling out fast, I move in front of her, lifting her face up, and she opens wide. Her violet eyes meet mine as I shoot my cum down her throat.

"Fuck, Catalina." I moan.

I watch her swallow and smile at me. "Thanks, baby." Licking her lips, she gets every last drop.

I bend down, kissing her deeply. "I love you, but don't think I brought you out on a date so I could get my cock wet. I wanted to spoil you because I love you. Let me untie you."

The worst part now is that I'll have to take her home. It was nice to forget about the stress of everything for a while. But now the real work begins.

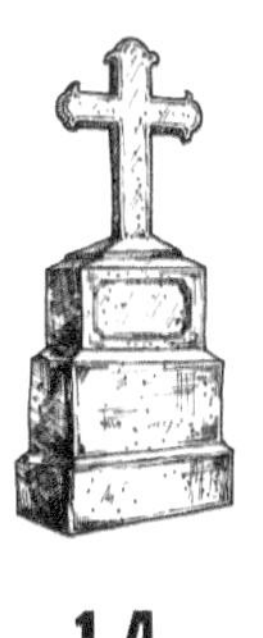

14

DORIAN

I won't lie. I'm glad Cole finally took Cat out for a date, but at a time like this? Going to Southside could've been dangerous. Sometimes, he doesn't think, which drives me up the wall. I'm glad Cat was safe, but we have six days until everything goes down.

I'm only worried about leaving a trail behind. I know Henry; if anything, he'll watch us all night. I'm unsure why he has us around if he can't trust us. It's been this way for almost a year, and it's getting tiresome. Nyx has the right idea about leaving the club. It's not worth it anymore. The benefits aren't there, and we've been treated like trash since Conrad joined.

The *family* Henry once thought he had is gone. I don't even know what we enforce anymore.

Unfortunately for us, Henry had called everyone in for another meeting before the official fun starts. The protocol is simple. He still wants everyone riding around the town's perimeter after sunset. I'm not sure why, it's going to be a madhouse, and there's nothing we can do about it. I hope he knows he just ruined this town.

"Everyone knows their job?" He looks around the table, and his eyes land on me.

"I think so. I mean, you are bringing more assholes into town, so expect murders, rape, and God knows what else. So have fun with the aftermath, but whatever." I shrug. It's not my fuckin' problem.

Conrad jumps out of his seat while Henry slams his fist on the table. The entire room falls silent. Cole and Nyx snap their heads at everyone else in the room. They wouldn't dare try anything.

Henry moves to me, getting in my face. "You're walking on thin ice, boy," he spits in my face. "I meant what I said earlier, and I'm a man of my word. Smarten the fuck up and do what I say." He turns to the room. "That goes for everyone here. If you don't want to be here, I can solve that. Do you think that cemetery is filled with town folk? Think again."

That's all the confirmation I needed. He and the Death Eaters also use the cemeteries as a dumping ground. Now, it makes me wonder if kidnapping Davis and Adams was a coincidence. Does Davis honestly get his dead body reports from the papers like he says?

"I want out after Halloween. I'm done with this shit." I stand to leave, followed by Cole.

"I want out, too. If Dorian and Nyx are out, then I'm gone. Sorry, Henry, but you've lost sight of everything since I joined. This isn't the family I want anymore. You best find new enforcers because your so-called club is shit."

That target on Catalina's back has just gotten more prominent; I can feel Henry's eyes burning into the back of my head as I leave, but what else can any of us do? Freddy meets us outside, looking sad.

"You boys leaving me, aren't ya?"

"Sorry, man, we can't stay here." I pull him into a hug.

He cradles the back of my head. "Don't worry. I'm sure you have plans, and I agree with them." He pulls away, hugging Nyx next. When Cole hugs him, it breaks my heart. He's like a grandparent, and Cole has never had one before. Freddy has always been there for us; our Sundays were the best.

"Don't worry, boys, this shit won't last long. I'll join you in retirement soon. That girl of ours needs me. She'll lose her mind if she has to hang around you assholes all the time."

Laughter poured from everyone.

"Fuck you, old man. I was born an asshole. I can't change," Cole chuckles.

Nyx nods. "That I'll agree on. Don't worry, we'll look after her."

My nerves have never been this close to the edge before. Cole still has no idea that Nyx and I planning on shipping Cat off to Riley's. We probably should tell Cat, too. Then again, we have time.

Looking at our front door, maybe we don't have time.

"What the fuck is this?" Cole rips the note off the door.

"What's it say?" Nyx crowds around, resting his hand on my shoulder.

Cole scans it before looking at us. His face grows paler the more he reads. I snatch the note, getting impatient.

If this is what a family looks like, you really fucked up. Good luck on purge night. K.

"Who the fuck is K?" Nyx takes the note, flipping it over.

That is what I would like to know. Conrad would do something like this; maybe he did and wrote a K to throw us off.

"Conrad," I growl.

Nyx thinks so hard his forehead lines crease deep. "There's no way. We left before anyone."

Cole paces the front yard. "He could've made anyone post it, but why the K?"

"Unless it isn't Conrad." Nyx stares at the note one more time.

"What makes you say that?"

"Think about it. Conrad doesn't do anything without Henry's say. Why would he post this before our meeting? Conrad is a coward. No one dares to come knocking on our door. Whoever this was has some major balls."

"Think it's someone from the school?" Cole questions, still staring toward the street.

"The question is, are we telling Catalina?"

"No," Nyx and Cole answer in unison.

That's what I figured. She's gonna hate us if she ever finds out that we are hiding something this crucial. "We hide it for now. If we get anything else, she needs to know. I'm not having a repeat of last year."

"Deal," Cole agrees.

Nyx nods. "I'll never place her in danger because we let our egos get in the way. But we need to figure out who K is."

"It has to be someone in the club that's pissed off with us for leaving." Recognition lit up in Cole's eyes. "Technically, Henry knew Nyx was leaving. Nothing stopped him from sending someone out here while we were gone."

He's not wrong. Nyx has made it known for a long time that he was leaving after Halloween—his time is almost up. I know it scared Henry at the thought of Cole and me leaving. Looks like he has everything to be worried about. Cole was right; it wasn't the family we first joined. It's funny that those were the words on the note.

"If it was Henry, then we take him out too." What's one more murder.

"Seriously, D. You want to kill two people in one night?"

"Don't act like we've never done it before, Nyx." I roll my eyes. He's a worry wart when he wants to be.

"That's different. We didn't have to kidnap them. We literally stormed the castle to kill them."

Cole scoffs. "Then we storm the castle and kill Henry, Conrad and Coleman."

"Woah." I hold my hand up. "Three, we're up to three now."

Cole shrugs. "Go big or go home, Dorian."

I can't believe I'm going to agree to this. If we want to clean up this town, there is no other way. We are enforcers and would be doing our jobs. One major loophole Henry didn't see coming. Now, we need a new plan for Coleman.

"Who's headed to watch Cat at school?"

"I will. I'm sure I'm stuck on dickhead duty still." Cole heads to his bike. "I'll send her home before heading out again," he calls over his shoulder.

Once his bike is down the street, Nyx and I are left to deal with his plan. How it will work is beyond me, but somehow, his plans always work, and I never think twice about doubting him.

"D?"

"Yeah, Nyx." I take him in. His face is serious, and disappointment shrouds his eyes when he turns to me.

"Do you think Cole is going overboard on the killings?"

"Coleman, yes. Not sure about Henry and Conrad. Then again, if we don't take them out, they could convince the next mayor or, even worse, run for it themselves. Who knows what they would do to this town."

He rubbed his hands on his thighs, shaking his head. "It's still bullshit, but whatever. If it helps you two and Catalina, I'm all in."

The resentment he houses for Henry will take years to get over. He still hasn't forgiven his father, and I don't blame him. Whenever I see Otis Thornton walking down the sidewalk, the need to hit him with my bike is strong. Can't believe that prick has the balls to walk around and act like he hasn't destroyed his kid's life.

I'm thankful that my so-called parents don't live here. The best thing to happen was for my grandmother to take me in. I miss her every day. Cancer can kiss my ass.

She's the one who taught me more than my own parents. They only wanted the status of having a child; the thought of raising me was too much. No matter what I was doing, they seemed to be pissed off with me. Not a single day went by that they didn't yell at me. I can't fault my Grandmother; she raised her son the same way she did me. Some grow up to be assholes.

With the reminder of my grandmother, I head inside to start dinner. Can't have my girl starving when she gets home from school.

15

CATALINA

There is something different with today. I can't place my finger on it, though, and it's driving me up the wall. All day in my art class, something in the back of my mind kept nagging me to check my car. I kept working on my sculptor and ignored it.

I could beat myself for being stupid. I'm beginning to think Johnny is cursed. Can spirits hitch rides? I'm starting to wonder if I brought one back, and it attached itself to my car. Bending to inspect the flat tire, I run my hand along it when I notice the puncture mark.

"The fuck?" I whisper.

Sticking my index finger in the hole. I haven't pissed anyone off this year. Okay, that's a lie, but Becky had it coming. There is only so much I can take before I snap, and she happened to find out the hard way. I'm not a slut for having three boyfriends. She kept telling everyone who passed her how I spread my legs for every guy on campus. No matter how often I would say no to her, doesn't make me a slut, and that's not how it works, she wouldn't stop. I'm glad Cole taught me how to throw a punch because that blow to her face was impressive.

This has to be her getting me back. "Fuckin' cunt."

"Who's a cunt?"

My head whipped around at the sound of Cole's deep voice. Exhaling, I point to my tire. "The cunt that did this, poor Johnny, has no luck with tires."

Cole moves behind me, squatting to examine my tire. Placing his hand on my back. "Sorry, Wednesday." His thumb brushed up and down my spine. "Do you have a spare?"

Angling my head to look up at him. He's wearing a black hoodie with his club cut over the top. A deep sigh escaped my lips. He always looks so well put together, even if it's for a bike ride. While I'm dressed in scrubby clothes today, I look like Elmer, the homeless guy. Cole's deep chuckle pulls me out of my thoughts.

"Yeah, sorry, the spare is in the trunk." Cole gives me the signal to pop my trunk because who wouldn't think of doing so. Rolling my eyes, I open my car door and press the button for the trunk. I shouldn't complain. This would take me hours to do. Cole rounds the front of the car with my spare.

"This won't take me long, but are you sure it was some-body you pissed off?"

The muscles in my jaw twitched with annoyance. "Who else could it have been? I'm sure I broke Becky's nose, so it would've been her."

He smirks as he jacks up my car. "Those private lessons paying off, are they?"

"When you don't have your hands all over my body, they work. But seriously though. Who else could it be? Don't fuckin' lie to me, Cole."

He's quiet while he finishes up with my tire. That's how I know it's not good news. It was only a matter of time before the truth came out. Makes me wonder how long the guys have been sitting on this.

He brushes his hand off on his jeans and throws the jack back into the truck. Bracing his hands on the bumper, his eyes collide with mine. "Wednesday. This isn't the place for this type of conversation." His voice lowered, and his lip curled into a snarl. "When we get to the house, we'll talk. Drive."

Go figure, he could never tell me shit without backup. I'm unsure what will change with having the guys around; I can already tell this will piss me off. Guarantee it has something to do with them following me around.

If they think I haven't noticed them acting weird since last week, they are sadly mistaken. Purge day is looming over us like the plague if I know them. I'll be kept away like a princess in a tower. They forget that I'm capable of handling myself.

When the house comes into view, my knuckles are white from gripping the steering wheel tight. Flexing my fingers, trying to get the blood flowing again. This conversation is already irritating me, and it hasn't even started.

"Out, now." Cole knocks on my window.

That man needs to learn patience.

The tension in the den is suffocating. I'm cool as a cucumber, sitting in the armchair waiting for anyone to speak. The only sound in the room is the clock ticking. Nyx stands by the fireplace with his hands in his jeans pockets. Not once making eye contact. When I look at Dorian, he's fiddling with his hoodie string. I mentally shoot daggers at him because he should've been talking first out of everyone.

Leave it to Cole to glare at me. I scratch my nose with my middle finger, getting a middle finger back in return.

"Can someone talk already?" I give them all one more look. "I'll tell you how this is going down. You three are going to work on Halloween night like you always do. You're all scared; I understand that. But treating me like a child isn't helping either. Stop keeping me in the dark."

"Fuckin' rights we care," Cole exploded. He rushes out of his seat, caging me into the couch. "Why the fuck do you think we keep doing what we do?"

I lean forward, almost touching his face. "I don't know? You don't tell me anything. For all I know, it's a way to control me."

He smirks. "You want me to control you? You would never leave this fuckin' house. Every time you do, something happens."

"I want you to start talking to me and treat me like a fuckin' equal."

He closes his eyes, resting his forehead on mine.

"Half pint, what Cole is trying to say is we are trying to protect you."

Cole hums. "Yeah, that." He kisses my forehead before backing away. "Sorry, but some things we leave out to save you the heartache."

Nyx still hasn't said a word, meaning there is more to say. Of course, this conversation couldn't be a simple one. They sure kept a lot hidden if they were still afraid to talk.

Nyx clears his throat. "We need you to stay with Riley on Halloween."

"Excuse me?"

"We won't be able to protect you, and we don't know anyone else you can stay with. Don't fight us, half pint."

I try to get up, but Cole pushes on my shoulder. "I don't like this idea either." He swings his head to the guys. "But they're right. Riley is your best bet," he grunts.

"Fine. I'll talk to him."

"Now would be nice. We don't have long." Nyx reminds me.

Cole hands me my phone, and I tear it from his hand.

Me: The three stooges need me to spend Halloween night with you if that works.

"Seriously?"

"It's rude to read others' messages. Cole."

Rye Rye: I don't mind. We can watch scary movies and plot revenge.

Me: Sounds perfect.

"He said it's fine."

"Good, I need to head out. Stay with these two."

Once Cole is gone, Nyx sits on the armrest. "Baby, we only do these things out of love. You know that, right?"

Dorian kneels in front, sliding his hand up my thighs. "We were only worried about what you would say."

What a lame excuse. They were only worried about getting their asses chewed out. Which I should be doing, but fuck, Dorian keeps sliding his hand further up my thigh, and it's getting hard to concentrate.

"How was school, baby?" Nyx runs his hands through my hair; closing my eyes, my head falls back.

"It was okay. It was after that sucked."

Dorian's fingers dip under my shirt, stroking my stomach, and I sink deeper into the chair. "How so? Us?"

Shaking my head. "No, someone stabbed my tire—"

"Excuse me." Nyx stands, eyes wide. "Were you hurt or anything?"

Dorian stops moving. "Half pint, this is serious. Was there a note or anything?"

My heart skids to a stop. No, this isn't the same as last year. My brother isn't coming back. He got what he wanted. These two are trying to freak me out so I don't do anything rash.

That's all that this is.

"Funny, I know what this is." I laugh, trying to get up. Dorian squeezes my sides.

"I'm not trying to be funny. Cole likes to hide shit from you, but things went down with the club. Cole and I are out after Halloween. Henry lost his shit and threatened you."

My cheeks heat from the rage that flows fast. Blowing out a breath, I try to control my words. "You don't think this was something I should've been informed of? Apparently, my time away did absolutely dickshit for you guys. Jesus Christ. Why must you keep me in the dark?"

"It was for your own—"

"Don't finish that sentence, Nyx." *For my own good*, I'm getting tired of hearing that. How is being kept in the dark for my own good? I'm at a greater risk of danger not knowing what to expect. I don't know what it is with these guys that they can't understand that.

"If it makes you feel any better, we did it out of love. We did what was best. At the time, we were scared, Catalina." Dorian backs away from me. "Don't hate us for trying our best."

"I don't hate you." Now I'm getting frustrated with them. "I'm having a hard time expressing what I mean here." Leaning over, I drop my head in my hands. "I just don't want what happened last year to happen again, is all. My car isn't an omen. It was a bitch from school, that's it, that's all. Now, I don't have work tonight. Give me a game plan for this evening."

Nyx sits back on the armchair, massaging my back. "If you say so, I believe you. But I swear to God, Catalina. The first sign of trouble this time, you call."

"I promise."

"Good, let's go make supper and watch a movie." Dorian heads out.

"Momma Bear is in a mood." Nyx jokes.

I can't help but laugh. I'm sure Momma Bear wanted to get lucky in the den.

16

NYX

One day until Halloween. The town is already on high alert. Most shops are prepping for one of the worst nights this town will ever see in their history. But who do you think allowed it? They did. They did nothing to stop it. Even now, no one has tried to boycott it. City Hall is vacant. The usual protestors are probably sitting at home, scared out of their wits, or excited. Honestly, it's hard to judge the people in this town. I'm not even sure about the surrounding towns ready to come in.

Henry made us come down first thing this morning for a debrief. Like I give a shit what he has to say. I ignored him; we had our own plans for tomorrow. He held his last meeting. There's not much I want to hear from him except three little words. *I was wrong.*

I park my bike outside of Riley's place. I need to have a talk with him before Catalina arrives tomorrow. I still don't trust this guy; it doesn't matter if they work together or not. We're putting all of our trust in him. If anything happens to her, he's a dead man.

His place isn't something I would be bragging about, but then again, he is a university student. I wouldn't have the place I have now without the guys. Banging on the door, I pray this asshole better be up. When he doesn't answer right away, I bang again. I'm sure his neighbours aren't too thrilled.

"Yeah, hold the fuck up," I hear him yell. The door swings open, and I'm greeted by a wild-haired, boxer-wearing man.

He better not be dressed like this when Cat is around.

"Can I help you?" he asks with a yawn.

"Riley?" I ask to confirm this isn't some stranger danger's house.

His eyes peel open slowly. "Yeah." He licks his lips and rubs his hand down his face. "What can I do for you? It's a little early?"

I raise a brow. "It's after nine." Then again, why are we talking about the time? "Yeah, um, I'm Nyx."

He blinks slowly as if the brain is computing information at a sloth speed. "Right, right. Catalina's boyfriend. Not the asshole one."

Good to know I don't hold that title. Makes me wonder how much Cat and Riley talk.

"I came by so we can talk about tomorrow."

He waves me off. "No need. This place will be like Fort Knox. No one will be getting in; if all else fails, we could go to the school. Whatever you think would be best."

He seems too eager if I say so. "Staying here will be fine. Get some fuckin' decorations so your place isn't attacked. I swear if anything happens to her, kiss your career goodbye."

He smirks. "Maybe you could be the asshole."

"You have no idea. She isn't the only one that knows how to dig a grave."

He gives me a slight nod before I turn away. I'm glad Catalina has a friend, but something tells me not to trust Riley. He seems like a decent guy and all, but my gut is being a nag. My gut has never steered me wrong.

Okay. Once when, Cole cooked that chicken, but that was completely different.

The last thing I want to do is add another body to our growing list. It's bad enough that our game plan for tomorrow is stressing me out. The thought of the mayor's bodyguards catching us is what worries me. But Cole keeps reassuring me they all know him. Getting into his house will be easy.

All I know is this nightmare will be a thing of the past in no time.

I take the long way home. The changing leaves were always my favourite thing about this time of year. Doesn't help that Eastwood is housed between winding roads, making it fun to speed through on the bike. Pushing my bike past the speed limit, the sound of the exhaust is music to my ears.

Passing the welcome sign, I make my way home. Having my freedom is great and all, but I need to spend more time with Cat. All this stress is weighing on me; only she can help me. Creeping down our street, I notice a white van parked across the house. I drive by slowly, studying the driver's side.

It wouldn't be weird if the driver's side wasn't empty. My radar is shooting red flares off. I quickly swing into the driveway and jump off my bike. Wasting no time, I run for the front door. Nothing else matters but getting to Catalina. My fingers tingle as I try to get the key into the lock; what if whoever was driving is in the house right now? I could be too late.

Trying to turn my brain off and not to think like that, the lock finally turns.

"Catalina!" I yell as I rush up the stairs. "Baby? Where are you?" Who cares if someone is in the house? Let them hear me. Reaching the landing, Cat stands with her bedroom door open, looking confused.

I rush to her, placing my hand over her mouth.

"Don't talk. It could be nothing, or we are currently being stalked."

Her violet eyes grow serious. She tries to mumble some kind of response from under my hand. With a roll of her eyes, she points to the window and throws her hands in the air.

"I'm not following."

"Mo, ssit."

I got that one. "Don't talk too loud." I drop my hand.

"Are you sure they aren't for the neighbour to rake the leaves?"

"I want to believe that, but when has Ms. Rita ever raked her fuckin' leaves, Catalina?"

"Touché. Have you called the guys?" She moves back into her room, closing her curtains.

Pulling out my phone, I open a group chat, sending the guys a quick SOS text. I move to her window and take a quick pic of the van. "You haven't noticed how long they've been there, have you?"

"No, you woke me up. I don't have morning classes today."

Probably a good thing. If she happened to go out, they might have followed her. All I can do now is wait until the guys show up—I'm not leaving Cat alone.

I make Cat crawl back into bed. There isn't much for her to do; the less she's walking around, the better.

"Did you search the house?" she whispers.

My head snaps toward her. "No. You were my concern." I scan her room, moving to her closet. Pulling the doors open fast only to be greeted by clothes. My chest falls in relief. That leaves the rest of the house.

"Lock the door behind me. Stay away from your window."

Not what I want to be doing. Then again, I need to make sure the house is safe. Checking all the rooms upstairs first, I head downstairs, listening for any unknown sounds. The house is silent as I make my way into the den. We should've invested in security, but we never had a single issue with someone trying to break in. The thought of us being a part of the club usually worked at scaring people away.

The jiggle of the outdoor handle has me freezing. Drawing my gun, I flick the safety off. My heart jumps in my throat with every step closer to the door. Moving the curtain away just enough to unlatch the lock. With one deep breath, I point my gun and open the door.

"Jesus Christ, Nyx. It's me."

"Fuck man, I would've shot you." I back up, letting Dorian inside and locking the door behind me. "Did you find anything?"

"Nah, man, it's all clear. Whoever parked out there must be trolling us. Cole is out checking the van."

"I didn't hear you drive up." I make my way to the basement.

Step by step, we listen for any sound. Dorian nods in the direction of the furnace room. Keeping my hand on my gun, I move closer. This is the last straw. I'm calling to get an alarm installed.

"Clear," Dorian calls out.

I check behind the furnace and hot water tank. "Same."

"You didn't hear us because we parked down the street. Figured an SOS meant trouble. Guess we were right."

Cole greets us at the head of the stairs. "Where is she?"

I point upward. "Locked in her room."

"Kitchen now."

This can't be good. Add him, not wanting Catalina to hear. Cole presses his palms on the island. The anticipation is killing me.

"The van doesn't belong to the club." His voice was calm but had an edge of stress to it.

"Are you sure?" Dorian looks like he doesn't believe Cole.

Cole runs his hand through his dark hair. "Yeah, we always install a tracker on our vans. This one didn't have one."

"Well, maybe they removed it."

Cole shakes his head. "Freddy is the one that installs them. I called and asked. He's never heard of this van before."

"Do you think someone is on to us?"

"Conspiring again, boys?"

Fucking hell. She doesn't listen. "And you can't listen. What did I say?"

"I waited, then I heard all you three gabbing like three mother hens. Figured it was safe to come down. The van is gone, by the way." She opens the fridge to grab a bottle of water.

We're up and moving to the front window. Where the hell was the creep hiding? Cole moves to the front door, cracking it open slowly. With a huge swing, he steps outside. I point to Cat, making her stay in the kitchen.

"Whoever it was also left a present," Cole says from outside.

"How bad of a gift?" Dorian calls back, never letting Cat see past him.

Cole walks back into the house, holding a yellow LED mask. Cat gasped, dropping her water.

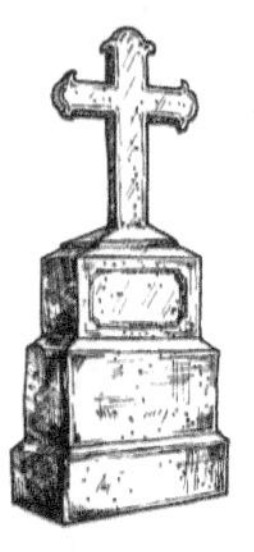

17

CATALINA

It's hard to breathe.

The grip on my throat won't loosen up. No matter how often I try to take a deep breath, the weight of what Cole brought into the house lands on me. That van belongs to only one person, but why the hell is he back?

The whole point of him terrorizing me last year was to get what he wanted, and he did. Why all of a sudden show back up again.

"I don't like this."

"Same, half pint. Why the fuck is he back?" Dorian hasn't left his spot by the window since our gift arrived.

Cole and Nyx haven't left my side. I'm not sure what this means for tomorrow night. If anything, it would be safer; as far as I know, my brother doesn't know anything about

Riley. I'm thankful that I don't have to work tomorrow. I'm not going through that again.

"It doesn't matter why he's back. We should've taken care of him when we had a chance." Cole's grip on my thigh tightens.

Nyx groans. "Cole, we can't add another body tomorrow."

"How many?" I dare to ask.

"Three," Dorian answers without a beat.

"Revenge requires more holes," I remind them.

Dorian smirks. "Good thing we know someone good at digging."

Oh, hell no. They can hit the road if they think I'm getting caught up in their shit. I won't even ask who they are killing because I don't want to know. Less is more in this case. I'll wait until the paper comes out, find out like everyone else, and pretend I'm not sleeping with the killers.

"Dorian, it's a good thing you can dig too." I shoot him a smug look.

"Don't worry, half pint, I wouldn't ask you to dig for us. I hope you aren't anywhere near what goes down tomorrow. I'm not even sure I want you to go to Riley's now."

"She can't stay here. Her brother knows she lives here," Nyx added. "Riley's is still the best bet."

Cole hasn't removed his hand or said a word. I'm afraid of what is going on in his head. If he thinks going after my brother will solve everything, he's wrong. More will only come. The only solution is to go after my mother. I need to figure out what the hell she wants. But being guarded all day tomorrow isn't going to help me get answers. Like hell, I'm calling. She doesn't need to know my number.

"Nyx is right. She'll still go to Riley's tomorrow as planned." Cole raises his chin, looking at me. "No arguing."

"Wasn't going to. I actually agree. If my brother returned, it can't be for a sibling reunion."

I hear him take a deep breath before releasing it slowly. Leaning over, he kisses me on the temple. "Thank you." He stands, digging his hands into his pockets. "We should get some scouting done before tomorrow, and I want everything to run smoothly."

Dorian studies me from across the room. "I'm staying with half pint. You, two, can handle this."

"Don't leave the house. We shouldn't be gone that long."

Nyx leans over, kissing my temple. "Be safe. Love you."

I watch them both leave, praying they will make it back. If my brother is still at large, who knows what will happen if he does find them?

"Don't worry so much, darling." Dorian strolls toward me, dropping to his knees.

"I can't help it. If he's out there, anything can happen, Dorian. What if he finds the guys?"

He rubs his thumbs across my bare knees. Never taking his eyes off mine, I've always loved watching his green eyes change from a light to a dark shade of green. He's such a beautiful man.

"You're beautiful too, darling."

"I need to stop talking out loud."

He smiles. "It's entertaining when you do. I never know what will fall from those lips." Slipping his hand under my thighs, I lift my ass off the couch so that he can pull my sleep shorts off.

"I'm so glad we never lost you," he whispers as he kisses the inside of my thigh. "Don't ever leave us again." He places his hands between my thighs, spreading them open. He lowers himself to the floor before moving between my thighs.

With one long, luscious lick, my body shudders in response. I can feel him smirk against my clit. Running my hands into his hair, I grab a handful, tugging his head back.

"Keep it up, and I'll fuck you instead."

"Works for me, darling." He moves away, undoing his jeans; he yanks them down his legs. His dick is hard and dripping in pre-cum. "Come fuck me."

I'm not sure which is wetter, my pussy or my mouth. Dragging my shirt off, the cool air feels welcoming on my skin. I watch as he tugs his shirt off and lies on the floor, giving his dick a few strokes. With a curl of his finger, he summons me closer.

Crawling on the floor, I work my way up his body. When I reach his hips, he grabs hold of me.

"I want to feel your pussy around my dick so fuckin' bad."

The need I have for him overwhelms me. I'll never be satisfied; living my entire life with him would never be enough. Even the afterlife wouldn't be ready for us.

I plant my hand on either side of his head and smile. "Don't move."

"Yes, ma'am." I lean down, running kisses along his jawline. His only response is making his dick twitch.

"I said don't move," I demand, moving my hand between our bodies and grabbing his dick. "Do I have to punish you?"

He groans in pleasure. "Fuck, no." Flicking my thumb over the tip, he hisses. "Please, Catalina." His fingers dig into my hips when I don't move, and his gaze holds mine as I slowly sink. Every inch working its way inside. Our moans grow loud until I'm seated on his body.

"Your pussy is already choking me—fuck, you feel so good like this."

I grind my hips, and my stomach tightens. I won't last long like this. The stimulation on my clit will push me over too soon.

"It's okay. Come for me."

Ah, fuck.

He grips my hips tighter, helping me move faster. Slapping my hand on his chest, my finger outlines the newest tattoo, a little tombstone. It's perfect.

The faster we move together, the more the world melts away. No one else matters.

"Catalina." Dorian moans. And that's my undoing. I'm not sure what it is about a man moaning, but fuck is it ever sexy.

My nails dig into his skin, and my toes curl.

"Don't stop moving. I'm coming too." He thrusts faster, bringing another orgasm out of me.

"Dorian, shit." Pulling me into his chest, he works until he's breathless.

With a long groan, he finishes, spilling deep inside of me. "God, I love you."

Cole and Nyx didn't make it home until late. I still didn't ask questions. Three bodies and scouting can't be a good thing. I have other things to plan. The number one obstacle is Riley. As I pack my bag, I try to think of a plan, but nothing comes to mind. Riley will be watching me like a hawk, and I guarantee going to the bathroom will involve him following me.

For now, I need to act casual or the guys will suspect that I'm up to something. Cole will sniff my bullshit plan out before I can plan it. The thought of seeing my mother again makes me sick. I'm older, and she can't control me anymore.

All I need to do is keep repeating that to myself until I believe it. Whenever I think of her, the little girl in me cowers more within.

Today is the day. Daddy is taking me shopping for my Halloween costume after school. He told me I could pick out whatever I wanted. Sitting at my desk, my brain can't think about anything else except what costume I want. All I want is to fit in with all the other kids. They dress up pretty every year, and I want that.

With a broad smile, Daddy meets me in the parking lot, and I know he's keeping his promise.

"Ready, sweetie?"

"Yep." I jump up and down with excitement.

His laugh grows loud. "Wonderful, what are you going to be?"

I tap my chin. "An Angel."

"Sounds wonderful. Let's get going before it gets too busy."

The store is busy, but I found what I was looking for. The best Angel costume that I've ever seen. I didn't even enter the house, and my mother ripped the bag from my hands. My hand throbs in pain, but I don't dare make a sound.

"What's this?"

"It's a costume. I didn't think there was any harm in it," Daddy tells her.

Her face scrunches up in disgust. "She doesn't need a fucking costume. She won't be going out on Halloween. What has she ever done to deserve that?"

She stares at me, and it eats away at me. No one will tell me why she doesn't like me. When she moves toward me, I hide behind Daddy.

I grip my sweater tight. That woman has no control over me anymore. Fuck her.

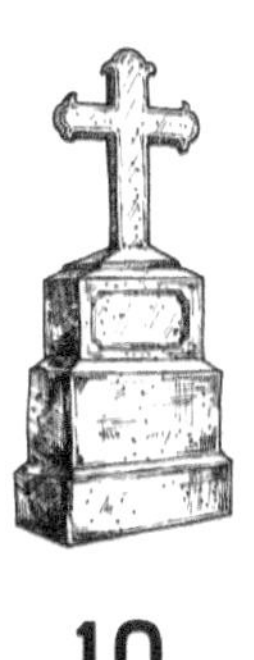

18

COLE

Halloween Day

The house is quiet as I make my way down both flights of stairs. I'll admit being on the top floor does get lonely. Catalina wanted her own room, and no one argued. We rotate rooms when she's up to it. I never want to intrude on her time, and it's been important to Nyx and Dorian.

It's hard to believe that tomorrow, this entire nightmare will come to an end. It feels like a decade since we heard about the stupid purge. I had to place my phone on silent. Henry kept blowing it up with pointless text messages. I'm not safe-guarding dick shit in this town tonight.

I head over to the patio doors and open the curtains. Taking a calming breath, our fuckin' guest came back throughout the night. All over the yard, red paint is splattered on the new patio set, the shed, and a trail leading up to the doors.

"Cole?"

"Yeah, Wednesday?" I don't bother turning around. I was hoping she wouldn't have to see this or the message he left.

"He's coming after me again, isn't he?" She speaks so low that I hardly catch it. This time, I turn around.

"No, he won't be able to find you. I swear on my life, Catalina. He won't get you again."

I read his message once more. *This time the clock won't strike before I do.* Written in red paint on the patio window.

By midday, Dorian is growing grumpy. He spent most of the morning cleaning the red paint off the shed; that shit didn't want to come off. Our shed, which once was black, is now stained red. If anything, it's a sign of what's coming.

"Come on, Cat. We don't have all day. I thought you packed last night?" My patience is running thin.

"Hold that pierced dick will, yeah. I'm grabbing one last thing," she calls down.

Definitely wearing thin. She doesn't make my life easier, that's for sure. Then again, it wouldn't be the way it is without her. She bounds down the stairs carrying her coffin-shaped weekender. Wearing her leggings and an oversized sweater, fuck she's beautiful.

"I'm ready. Who's driving?" she asks, heading to the front door.

Dorian grabs her bag. "I'll be driving. Cole and Nyx will be on their bikes, Cole leading and Nyx bringing up the rear. They will intercept at any sign of trouble, and I'll get you out of there. No one needs to know where you are headed. Any questions?"

She slips her boots on. "Only one."

"We're listening."

"What if he isn't working alone this time around? We have no idea why he's back."

Nyx pulls her into his chest. "Shh, nothing will happen. If that prick shows his face, we will deal with him."

"All we need you to do is have fun at Riley's and not think about tonight," Dorian adds.

I place a hand on her shoulder. "Let's go, Wednesday."

I didn't think this would be hard. Driving in front of the SUV, scanning every side road for a white van. I thought for a moment as we passed main street, I spotted it. It turns out it was a stupid delivery van. My mind is playing tricks on me. I hope Cat isn't stressing. Knowing Dorian, he'll make her feel at ease. The windows are blacked out so that even if her brother were to spot us, he wouldn't see her.

Riley's place is only a few blocks away when I spot a white van parked down an alley. I signal Dorian to keep going, and Nyx pulls up beside me.

"What's going on?"

I climb off my bike, nodding to the van. "I'll check it out. Stay here and make sure you can still see Dorian."

"Call out if you need me. Who knows what he's capable of."

I hope it's nothing and it's a random van. There's no way he was able to follow us, slowly creeping down the road. I stick close to the apartment building; you would've missed him if you weren't looking. He parked behind the dumpster, only his front end showing. It seems like the same van; then again, it has no distinctive marks to go by. Peeking through the driver's window, I see fast food wrappers spread across the passenger seat and spilling onto the floor. This wouldn't be his van unless her brother had eaten his weight in food in the last twenty-four hours.

Nyx is scanning the street when I reach him. "I don't think it's his." Mounting my bike, I take a look down Riley's street. Dorian parked across from his house.

"For sure?"

A nagging feeling in my gut appears. "Not one fuckin' bit, Nyx. But what the hell are we supposed to do?" I start my bike, which roars to life, ending the conversation. I need to make sure Catalina gets into that house safely before the shit storm arrives tonight. I'm hoping the visit Nyx gave Riley was enough to scare him. If not, the coincidences are going to suck for him.

Dorian meets us outside of the SUV, looking down the road. "I take it you didn't find him."

"Nothing. Move her fast to be safe." I rush across the street, pounding on the front door.

Riley pulls it open, looking nervous. "You guys love knocking loud, don't you."

"Later, have you noticed anything weird in the area lately?"

His brows pinch. "Ah, no. Nothing out of the norm. Why?" his voice rises.

I wave Dorian over. They cover Cat as they rush her across the street. Surprisingly, they didn't carry her.

"What's going on?" Riley asks once Cat makes it up the stairs.

She laughs. "It's Halloween. Get that fuckin' pumpkin outside." Riley mumbles under his breath but does what she says. Rules are rules, and decorated houses are safe in this town.

We all crowd in his front entrance, getting our good-byes in.

"Be safe tonight, all of you. I mean it. I won't be able to dig enough holes for the massacre I'll create. It'll be a cremation in the middle of town."

Her eyes bounce between ours, and I can feel the passion spilling from her words. I believe every one of them. She would kill for us, just like we would for her.

"Nothing will happen to us, baby." Nyx presses his lips to hers. "I promise."

"We always keep our promises, don't we, half pint." Dorian cups her head, tipping it back. She gives him a small smile. "Now kiss me." With a roll of her eyes, she lifts her toes, pressing her lips to his.

She wraps her arms around my neck, tugging me down. "I hate that you're so tall."

"I'm sure you do, except when you try to reach the mugs every morning."

"That's one reason why I need you to get back. How am I supposed to survive without coffee?" Her eyes tear up.

"You could lower the shelf, or we could get a mug tree." Wiping away a stray tear, she tries to smile.

"The mug tree sounds cool." I smash my lips to hers. I can't take her tears anymore. She's supposed to be the strong one.

"I love you, Wednesday. We'll go shopping when we get back."

"Promise?"

"Always."

Only a couple of hours until the night starts. We have some prep to take care of before we technically have to show ourselves at the compound. The first thing is to dig some holes in the cemetery. I'd rather have that ready to go, so dumping is quicker.

No one likes to be caught with their pants down.

We decided on Eaglewood; being away from everything tonight would be the best. Although we aren't sure how that will go this year, outsiders might find it too. God, this year is such a mess.

I'll admit Eaglewood is a pleasant cemetery. The massive iron gates that welcome you as you drive down the road are once said to keep the souls locked in, or that's the rumour that was spread around elementary. Oak trees guard the surrounding property as far as the eye can see; some are as old as the cemetery, which dates back over a hundred years. But the best part is the entry road that circles the cemetery hides old and new gravesites. It's like an Easter hunt looking for old tombstones. Mausoleums are mixed within, housing the rich folks of Eastwood.

It's indeed a sight to see. Too bad assholes will be buried here tonight.

I park at the very south of the cemetery along the treeline. This is where some of the oldest graves are.

"This should do it. They shouldn't mind new bunk-mates."

Nyx looks pale. I guess he still can't handle this part.

"I'm sure the bodies are gone, bud. You can't even read the tombstone anymore." Dorian rubs the stone to prove it. "We won't even go down that deep, yeah?"

He swallows, lip curling. "Yeah, okay. But I'm shooting Conrad."

Whatever makes his little heart happy. But it can be satisfied after the work is done. We need to dig three holes before Henry figures out shit. I'm surprised he hasn't called yet; wondering where we are. Usually, he can't keep out of my life.

The first few hits to the dirt remind me why I hate doing this. Are we even gonna have the energy for tonight?

"What are we doing after?" Nyx wipes his forehead, panting. Someone needs to visit the gym more.

"I guess we have no choice but to listen to whatever bullshit Henry has to grace us with. Then we wait and strike."

Dorian stares off. "The quicker we do this, the faster we can get back to half pint."

"Agreed. Finish up, and we'll get out of here."

I can't wait to see the look on Coleman's face when he realizes it's his last purge, and it isn't how he expected it to go. No pussy for him tonight.

19

DORIAN

One last purge. That's what I keep telling myself the entire time as I dig this hole. The mantra of the night, I feel. Whoever rooms in this hole better enjoy it. And lord have mercy on anyone's soul that finds these pricks.

The hours are ticking by, and we should do more than digging. But prep work is essential, and I get that, but fuck. The anticipation for tonight is killing me, plus leaving Cat alone. I don't fully trust Riley.

"We about done or what?" Nyx calls out from his hole. "I swear I saw a bone."

"Pussy," Cole yells back. "How can you kill someone but can't do this? Seriously, I wonder about you some days."

Nyx groans, followed by a loud thump. "I'm done. I can't do this anymore."

I stand, getting a better view, and his shovel lies on the ground outside the hole. Nyx is halfway out of the grave, covered in dirt.

"Honestly, they don't deserve to be buried any deeper. Call it quits, Cole." Bracing myself, I hop out. The three graves lie waiting, side by side.

Cole's phone rings, sending my heart rate flaring. In a way, I hope it's Cat, but I know it's Henry. It's time.

We swing by the house and clean up; the less suspicion we give away, the better. Three hours until the purge commences. I stand in the driveway, watching all the innocent kids go door to door, trick or treating as their parents scan the road. This isn't what this night is meant to be. How can kids be kids if danger is lurking hours from now? A little boy spots me from across the street, and his face lights up; he's dressed like a biker, and I wave him over. His parents look nervous but must notice the patches on Cole and Nyx's back because the kid comes rushing over.

"I love your bike," he squeals.

I bend down, resting my hand on my seat. "Did you want to sit on it?"

His eyes shine bright. "Can I really? It's so big."

"Place your foot on the peg and your hand on the gas cap; one big pull, and you'll be up." He does what I say, and I lift him by his vest, getting him seated. His parents watch but never get closer.

"Wow, this is so cool. I can't believe you get to ride this all the time."

I laugh; his enthusiasm is welcoming tonight. "One day, kid, you can too."

"Cody, we should get going before it gets too late," his mom calls.

"Thank you, mister." He struggles to dismount, so I lift him using his vest. He runs straight to his parents. He leaves bouncing and talking up a storm.

"Nice, Dorian. That kid will have good memories for tonight." Cole pats my back.

"He'll get all the babes now and probably be a player come high school." Nyx laughs.

At least there won't be an MC for him to join.

The ride through Eastwood during fall is beautiful. You wouldn't know that it houses a large university. The small-town feel is what initially brought my grandparents here. It's also the thing that drove my parents away. They didn't like that everyone knew your business or the lack of shopping centres. For me, it was perfect. After Grandmother died, I sold her house. I couldn't bear living in it still—too many memories in the walls. A wonderful family bought it, and I'll drive by every once in a while.

"Dorian, how many times do I have to tell you not to play in the street? You and Nyx are going to get run over." Grandmother stands on the porch, trying to look mad. But Nyx and I both know she won't yell at us.

Nyx and I look at each other, trying not to laugh. "Grandmother, the street is empty. Besides, we move the hockey net when a car comes. We aren't babies anymore."

"Yeah, Mrs. Prescott. Sorry about your luck, but we are teenagers now."

Grandmother shakes her head. "You two will be the death of me."

She got diagnosed with cancer that year. She joked we caused it. She would roll over in her grave if she knew what I was doing now.

The compound is busy as we roll in; every member is here tonight. The only one I don't see is Freddy. Red flags sound off; he would've told us if he had left already. Something isn't right. Cole pulls next to me, scanning the crowd. But it's Nyx that speaks.

"Where's the old man?"

I keep scanning the area, hoping I overlooked him. It can't be that hard to find an old man. Not a sign of him. Only Henry and Conrad stand tall, smiling and waving at all those suckers.

"I can't find him. Do you think Henry told him to stay home?"

"God, I hope so. If he did anything to him. His death will be painful and fuckin' slow." Cole hasn't taken his eyes off Henry. "We better head over before he has an aneurysm."

The walk through all the guys usually feels like an accomplishment. This time, I feel like an enemy walking amongst them, wondering if they know our plans. The only one that does isn't here. I want to say if there were any signs of trouble, Freddy would've called. He is stubborn, but not like that.

Henry sees us and grins. Asshole.

"Shoot me now. This speech is going to make my ears bleed. I can already feel it." Nyx stepped forward, hate gleaming in his eyes.

Cole stands next to me, arms crossed. "Let the bullshit fly." He speaks from the corner of his mouth.

Henry takes in the crowd almost like he's satisfied. He claps twice. A hush falls upon us all. And the prick looks pleased. President or not, he lost my respect.

"Welcome, everyone." The crowd claps, minus us three. "Yes, it is a time to celebrate. Coleman would've been here, but he is prepping for tonight. Now, our job is to ensure the town is safe, especially since it's open to the public this year. You are all aware of your jobs. Do you have any questions?"

Nyx goes to raise his hand, but Cole stops him. Royce lifts his. "I have one. What's the whole point of this purge night?"

The million-dollar question. Will he tell the truth or not?

Henry chuckles, a clear sign he won't tell the truth. That Coleman wants free sex without paying for it. So he would rather chase after an innocent woman and rape her. What a great so-called purge.

"The mayor wanted to try something new a few years back and called it a purge. I'm not sure why; it had nothing to do with purging. This year, he decided to have no rules; anything is open."

Royce doesn't look convinced. "Aren't the town folk concerned about all the murders and rape going on in town?"

"Listen here, boy. It's his town, not yours. Follow the rules, got it? Don't talk back." Henry's face turns a lovely shade of crimson, and it's comical. Someone finally had the balls to call him out on his shit.

Conrad steps forward, pointing to the far end of the compound. "Meeting's over. Go do your job."

Fun sucker.

He dies first, last to join first out. I don't make the rules, but I'll follow them in this case. I glare at the two cunts. Tick Tock, and then it hits me—Catalina's brother's warning from this morning. He said the clock won't strike when he does. The last time he struck was when the clock downtown was broken at twelve. Who the fuck knows this time. We need to get this done now.

Me: How is it going?

It's only been a few hours, but I need to confirm that she's doing okay.

Half pint: All good on the front. You?

Me: Not giving you details. But let's say Henry gave us his lame speech, and we didn't die from boredom.

Half pint: Thank God for that. Who would get me off if you did?

Me: Cat, I can't be walking around with a hard-on.

Half pint: Haha, it would be funny. I better go. Riley has the popcorn ready. Movie night starts soon. Please be careful. Love you, tell the guys.

Nyx nudges me. "What's wrong?"

"Hmm? Oh, nothing. Cat says she loves you guys."

"What else did she say?"

I let out a sigh of relief. "They are watching a movie and eating popcorn. Didn't mention anything else, which is good."

He bites his lower lip. "Yeah, or they haven't noticed it yet. The quicker we do this, the faster we get back."

The only other problem is Henry and Conrad are still hanging around, watching us. It's like they are trying to figure out why we are still here. It would be easier if they walked into the end of my gun while I pulled the trigger.

"Head for the bikes. Make it look like we're headed for our corner of the town. Once it's seven, we'll come back for these two." Cole salutes them before walking to his bike.

I leave without giving them any sort of acknowledgment.

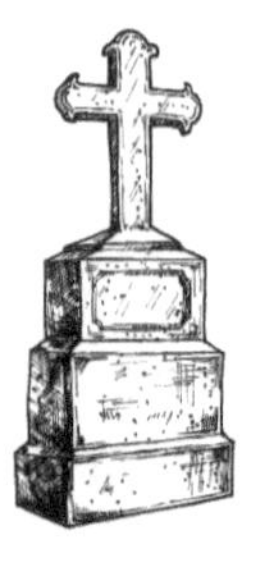

20
CATALINA

I've been watching my clock, which is pointless; you'll know when it's seven. Minutes before, it'll be quiet and then all hell will break loose. I watch Riley check the window, and he sucks in a deep breath. I jump out of my seat, rushing to his side; gripping his arm, we watch the street flood with people wearing all sorts of masks.

"Jesus fuck." I watch as they carry weapons of all shapes and sizes—from machetes to baseball bats.

"I've never seen this before, Cat."

I move away, double-checking the front door, not that it matters. If anyone wanted in, a deadbolt wouldn't be stopping them.

"Riley, close the curtain and turn the lights off."

I turn the TV off, making the entire house dark. Maybe hiding at the school would've been the wiser choice. Then again, I didn't expect this. The noise begins to pick up, and screams echo between the walls. Riley pales.

"We need to hide," I whisper.

He nods, pointing down the hall.

"We can hide in my closet. Do you think they got my neighbour?" His hand freezes on the closet handle.

My heart breaks. I hope not, but anything is possible tonight. "Let's get inside."

I thought I was scared when my brother kidnapped me, but this is much worse. These people won't think twice about killing or doing anything to you. They won't get punished for it. Unlike Cole, Dorian and Nyx, they asked if I wanted it. Whoever comes through that front door won't ask. I don't even think a simple Halloween decoration will stop them.

Riley squeezes my hand, it hasn't been over ten minutes, and the night is growing louder. If only the guys expected this, I could've been more prepared. I don't think anyone knew what to expect with more people joining. What the fuck was the mayor thinking? Did he want everyone in town killed?

"Cat, if we don't make it out of this—"

"Shut that cake hole. We will."

He sighs. "But if we don't, having one friend is nice," he says, the vulnerability in his voice.

I shift, feeling for his shoulder. I pull him closer. "As much as I hate working inside and with other people, working with you isn't that bad. Now, grow a pair. We ain't dying."

He laughs. "If you say so."

At least we aren't dying today. Not by some asshole in a hockey mask. If anything, I'll do the killing with a hockey stick.

I'm not sure how long it's been. My dumbass left the phone in the living room. I'm certain Riley has covered his ears; the screaming has gotten to him. I thought for sure that it would've moved on by now, but they keep coming. We have until the morning to deal with all this shit.

"Stay here. I have to grab my phone."

"I'll come. You shouldn't go alone."

We slowly make our way down the hall; an orange glow flickers behind the curtains as we round the corner. I feel Riley tense next to me.

"Where were you last year during the purge?"

"I went to my mom's. She has a cabin a few hours away."

I dig my fingers into his forearm, taking his focus away from the window. "It wasn't like this, I swear. This is new to me, too."

"I think we should get to the school."

And I still need to get my ass to deal with my brother and mother. But I can't leave Riley alone; the poor guy wouldn't survive. I point my finger at him to stay. I stick to the shadows, getting close to the window. If we can leave the house without being spotted, we have a better chance of getting out of the neighbourhood.

I grip the curtain, taking a deep breath. The uncertainty of what lies behind them has a chokehold on me. But saving the guys is more important, and finding my brother is do or die. Moving the curtain enough that I can peek through, the street comes into view.

The neighbour's place across the street is trashed. The entire front of the house is spray painted, and the windows are broken. They had the nerve to toss the furniture outside. A small fire is burning in a barrel in the middle of the road, six feet away from another. I think another house is destroyed with a fire burning in the driveway. I feel sorry for the person who didn't park their car. It's now upside down.

People are still milling around, covered in blood. They seem to be patrolling the street like bodyguards.

"All right. We have three groups of five. All have weapons, and not one has a gun, so that's a bonus."

Riley laughs. "How so?"

"They can't shoot us while we run." And not a single person is wearing an LED mask. So he's not out there.

I head into the kitchen, pulling the silverware drawer open.

"Have you ever killed anyone before, Cat?"

"No, but that doesn't mean I won't. Find a weapon, Riley, and look confident when holding it."

He holds his hand out. "I use a knife in the lab. You should find a different weapon."

He has a point and probably has better luck locating veins than I do. With his help, I'm wielding an aluminum baseball bat. This will work perfectly.

"How do we get out of the house?" Riley peeks through the backdoor blinds. "They are everywhere. There's a fire out here, too."

What can we do? We are both victims if we leave like this. Riley heads to the living room, and I search the kitchen for something. I need a sign, and I'm almost ready to pray if I have to.

"Think Catalina, what would Lucy do?"

"Who's Lucy?"

"Um, Lucifer." I roll my eyes. How do people not know that?

"I don't think that's the saying. But I found these." Riley holds up two ski masks. Fuckin' ring-a-ling.

I swipe mine. "Told you praying would work."

"Ah, you didn't."

I raise my brow, and he doesn't need to know shit. I quickly braid my hair before tugging on my mask—this better work.

With a slightly panicked look on his face, I unlock the backdoor. "Walk casually until we can't, then run. Don't let go of my hand."

He nods. My heart is choking me. Never in my life did I think this would happen again. It's another nightmare, and I can't control it. Riley's hand tightens around mine, and cracking the door open, the cool air hits me. What was once filled with a crisp smell is now filled with burning wood and something else I can't figure out.

The coast is clear, and we slip out of the house; moving at a fast-paced walk, we get into the alleyway, and it's a murder scene. I weave my fingers between Riley, moving fast. Pools of blood lie all over the pavement; I'm afraid to look at the bodies, praying it's not someone I know. The revenge people have to do this is unreal.

"Jesus," Riley mutters under his breath.

We make it to the main street before we are spotted.

We might as well have a neon sign pointing at us. More people come out between the shops. The only thing saving us is we are the strangers of the crowd. They have no idea who we are. I have no hard feelings when I bash their heads in with this bat.

I twirl the bat in my hand. Riley stands tall, holding the knife away from his body, waiting for his victim.

"Well, what do we have here?" some slutty doll says. Can we pick any more of an original costume for Halloween? Her little group of slut dolls giggle. Gross.

Riley groans. I feel his pain. "Just nick the artery and let them bleed out."

He side-eyes me. I shrug. Lifting my bat, the head it is, then.

The slut dolls crowd around us, and then the wanna-be horror killers to do. Being in the middle of a murder circle doesn't feel like it would. Riley has his back to mine, and his heart is beating as fast as mine. We slowly turn. Clutching my bat, I try to think of a game plan. The horror killers are men and will undoubtedly be harder to take down.

"Go after the girls. We need a pathway."

"Lord forgive me."

"I'm sure Lucy will welcome you with open arms."

He releases a deep sigh. "Not funny."

It's either now or we both die here. I step forward, and the air shifts. Don't fail me now, Riley. Without thinking, I rush forward to the first person to my right. With a giant swing, I wait until my bat connects with a body part.

A deep chuckle is all I get in return.

"I think you missed little girl."

Shit.

The ass wearing the hockey mask steps closer, his knife dripping blood. I swing again, aiming low. He yells out in pain.

"Didn't miss that time, prick." I swing once more. The cushion of his head silences the hollow ping from the bat. "Sorry."

I try not to pay attention to the blood spilling from his head or how it was a kid from school. Nope, just keep plowing through the bodies, Cat. Don't think about it—keep going.

I bend down to grab his knife just as a gust of wind blows over my head. Holy shit balls. I turn over, and it's a slut doll. She giggles.

"I almost had you, don't worry. She will."

Her words barely register before the sharp pierce to my right shoulder comes. "Fuck," I hiss, trying to reach the knife that's sticking out of my shoulder. My fingers shake as I try to touch the handle, and my stomach flips. I've cut myself plenty, but I have no words to compare it to this.

"It's a shame about your friend too."

Riley. No, she's lying. He's fine; he has to be. "Fuck you," I spit out. Slowly getting to my knees, I reach for the knife from hockey boy. The bitch that stabbed me steps forward, eye for an eye doll. I wait until she's right before me; this knife better be sharp.

One smooth slice and the knife sinks into the Achilles tendon of her left foot. She falls, screaming; the other doll helps to stop the bleeding. I try to stand, but my shoulder screams in pain. I need to find Riley. Trying again, I clutch my arm and stumble upward, biting hard in pain. I'm surprised I didn't break my molars.

The street is madness. What I thought were teams have now turned on each other. The distraction is welcoming if only I could find the person I needed. No matter where I turn, I can't locate him. Did he make it out?

I don't want to leave without confirming, but staying here isn't an option. My body jerks forward, a hand clenching my bad shoulder.

"Cat, we have to run."

I take Riley in. His ski mask is covered in blood splatter. I examine his body for any wounds. "You hurt?"

"No." His eyes focus on the blade. "Cat, Jesus. We need to go."

Thank God, because I don't think I could make it there alone.

21

NYX

I'm pissed when we pull out of the compound. Playing nice is one thing, but to stand there and watch all that shit play out tonight was wrong. What a stupid speech. I still can't believe out of everyone there, only Royce had the balls to stand there and speak out. If Henry wasn't on the kill list, Royce wouldn't see the end of the week.

As we drive through town, you can feel the shift. We take the outer road that leads to the high school, and people dressed in costumes already begin to enter the town. Who knows where they parked and if they will ever return to their cars. I am not on clean-up duty this year. Thank fuck for that.

I follow Cole and Dorian into the school parking lot. This night is gonna be one big nightmare.

"We'll double back for the compound. I think it's best to park the bikes at the gravel pit and sneak through the trees."

I like Cole's plan, but. "What if they left the compound?"

"Nah, those two are cowards. No worries there." Dorian winks.

"Figures. They're all for this shit, but can't even take part—" A blood-curdling scream fills the sky, cutting me off. Shivers snack down my spine.

That's not a good sign and a sound I never want to hear. I'm glad we left Cat with Riley safe inside. I can't imagine having her anywhere near this shit. She never needs to see what mess the town turned into.

"Let's roll before some ass decides to kill us. I have no idea how Henry thought we could control this." Cole shakes his head.

"Fuckin' hopes and dreams, man," D scoffs.

Even the back way to the compound is worse than playing a game of dodgeball. Every few feet, a dick in a mask would jump out in front of us, swinging their weapon, trying everything they could to slice our hands or legs. Barrels line the middle of the streets, burning what I hope is wood scraps. But I wouldn't put it past anyone if a body was burning instead. The stench is dead on.

The gravel pit was abandoned years ago, and the Soul Stealers took over it as a shooting range. At the odd time, teenagers will use it for parties, but that also involves someone coming to the compound and asking permission.

As suspected, it's vacant. Even during a purge, no one is stupid enough to come out here, even to hide. Climbing off my bike, I open my side saddle. We packed the essentials before leaving the house earlier—Our masks.

"Are you guys ready?" Yet again, who placed Cole in charge?

I cock my gun, sticking it back in my pants. "I'm good."

We wait for Dorian to answer. "D?"

He climbs off his bike. "Yeah, I was thinking of Catalina. You believe she's safe?"

I keep telling myself she is. If not, I'll go insane.

"She's fine. If anything happened, she would call." Cole walks away, shutting the conversation down.

I'll chalk it up to the stress of his short temper, not because that's who he is. Or the fact that we are under a lot of pressure.

We track through the bush, staying out of view of the compound's cameras. The closer we get, the faster my pulse races. I never thought this day would come, and leaving the club would bring me the freedom I needed. Turns out it was killing the president and vice president.

When we break the tree line, the compound comes into view. Cole gives us a signal to go left and stay low. We need to gain access through the torture room. It's the only room without an alarm, a fault all on its own. It's not like I was ever going to say anything. It was handy when we dragged a body in and didn't have to worry about punching in a stupid code.

Lining up on the property line, we watch and listen. It's so dark; the clouds are covering the moon, working in our favour.

"Once inside, no one talks. Knowing Henry, the alarm will be set, and we have ten seconds before it beeps when we exit the room; if my assumptions are correct, he should be in his office. Conrad will be in his room with a hang around." Cole directs us like the leader he is. "One more thing," he adds. "Get out alive." He sticks his mask on.

I place my mask on. "Got it," I answer.

"Yep," Dorian agrees, sticking his mask on.

That's my main goal tonight: getting back to Catalina alive. If I come back like a slice of Swiss cheese, it doesn't matter. It's better than not breathing.

"Move out," Cole grinds out.

We scurry across the parking pad and the small yard. Resting against the garage wall, we double-check our surroundings. I watch the main entrance. Why wouldn't he have it guarded? Especially tonight of all nights. I take a step toward the compound.

The air cracks with gunfire, and before I can register it, the dirt in front of my foot flies upwards. Cole pulls me back against the building.

"Looks like someone is onto us," he hisses.

"No fuckin' shit," I pant. "I think I shaved off ten years of my life."

Dorian reaches for his gun. "Gunfight it is. My guess is Conrad."

Yeah, cause his aim is shit, plus Henry doesn't enjoy getting his hands dirty. We learnt that the hard way. I grab my gun, bending down to grab a rock. Time to see where the fucker is hiding. Cole nods, letting me know he's ready. My guess is he's hiding inside, shooting from the bedroom window. Pussy.

The third window in, the curtain moves. Bingo had a baby, and his name is... I throw the rock fast and hard. It shoots right through the window, and you can hear him yell.

"Move fast," Cole bellows.

We book it across the lot, flattening against the compound building wall. The door we need is only feet from us. Bending low, we move, Cole in the front and Dorian taking up the rear. I have no problem being the middleman. Commotion is happening within the compound's walls, guaranteeing Conrad has found Henry.

The door we need finally comes into view, and I'm unsure if relief is the word that comes over me or anticipation. The battle is only beginning.

"Light 'em up. I can't say what's expected, but shoot to kill." Cole turns his mask on, eliminating the night with a blue haze.

"It's gonna be a shit storm," Dorian says. Turning on his mask.

I just flick mine on, adding the green to the mix. I need one good shot. I'm over the thought of torturing these pricks. Cole rushes through the door first, and I pursue.

As expected, the inside is dark, but voices are heard, and they are panicking.

I've always enjoyed an excellent cat-and-mouse game.

"We know you're here. What do you want? We aren't taking part in the purge." Henry calls, his voice cracking.

That's right, be scared.

"I mean it, don't you know where you entered? This is the Soul Stealers. I can have you killed, and no one would care." He continues.

I think I figured out where he's hiding. I nudge Cole, nodding in the direction of the bar. Conrad is quiet. Your time will come, my pussy friend.

Circling the bar, Henry hasn't even noticed our presence yet. He's still yelling at us to leave him alone. It isn't until Cole laughs and Henry shuts up.

"Cole?" His head swivels, taking all of us in. "Dorian, Nyx?"

"Sorry, man, but no hard feelings, yeah?" That sounds sincere to me. If he's lucky, I won't spit on his grave.

"I did everything for you boys and this is how you repay me?"

"You didn't try to stop this from happening to the town. Have you even been out there to see what has happened so far? It's a gong show. A fuckin' nightmare, and for you to think we could protect anyone is unrealistic. You have your dick so far up Coleman's ass I'm surprised you can still piss. You are a disgrace to this town." Cole raises his gun. "I can't believe I looked up to you at one point."

Henry backs up, raising his hands in surrender. "Please."

"Nah, the fact that you still don't get it makes this easy." Dorian raises his gun, too.

I glare at Henry; something is still eating at me. "Where is Freddy?"

He laughs. "That old fuck? He didn't want a part of the club anymore. Said his old body couldn't handle it anymore. I told him to get the fuck out of here."

"Is that all? How did you know an attack was coming tonight?" I press for more; that ass is holding back, I know it.

He shrugs. "Maybe I made him talk, and there's no way he didn't know shit about tonight. Someone doesn't quit out of the blue."

I clench my teeth hard—that asshole. I leap over the bar, punching Henry in the face. "You prick. Do you feel like a big man, beating the shit out of an old man?" I slam my fist into his eye. It's not like he'll need to see again. He groans in pain, but it's not enough.

"I'm gonna fuck you up like you did to this town." Fuck, taking it easy. I grip his shirt, dragging him out from behind the bar; he scrambles to stop me, but I'm stronger when I'm pissed.

I toss him on the floor, kicking him in the ribs. He rolls onto his side, coughing. Grabbing his hair, I look into his non-swollen eye. Horror seizes him; he's not the man I once knew. I'm looking into the eyes of a coward. Releasing him hard, his head bounces off the floor. My fist flies; I can't tell you where it lands. All the anger I have housed inside is being released. My parents still won't give me the time of day, and honestly, if someone got them tonight, would I care? Would they care if I didn't make it? Over something that happened years ago.

A hand squeezes my shoulder, pulling me from my thoughts. I look down, and Henry is a mess. My hand is a swollen, bloody mess.

"He's gone, Nyx," Dorian reassures me. "You okay?"

I take a couple of deep breaths, nodding. "I will be. One down."

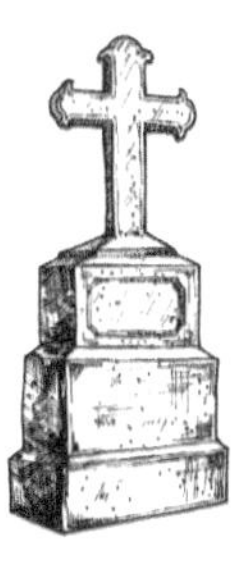

22

COLE

I watch in horror as Nyx beats the shit out of Henry. The laid-back, reserved guy I grew up with since junior high is kneeling over Henry, using his fists as a weapon. Never in my life would I have thought I would witness this. I'm at a loss for words.

He's so disengaged from his surroundings that I wouldn't be surprised if he had no idea what was happening.

"Dorian, stop him before he regrets everything about tonight." I can't let him go much longer. He'll never recover.

Nyx sinks onto his heels, looking at his hands. The glow from his mask made the blood glisten.

"Shit," he mutters.

"You okay? And don't give me that bullshit answer. I'm *fine.* Seriously, what's going on in your head?"

He takes a deep inhale. "I was thinking of my parents and how it was so easy for them to forget about me."

"Nyx, you don't need them. It's been three years, and they haven't tried. We're your family." Dorian grips his shoulder. "We need to finish what we started."

Conrad, where is that snake? I'm surprised he didn't try shooting us from behind.

"Yeah, I'm good. Sorry for going off track."

I laugh and shrug. "Well, it wasn't the shootout, but he's dead." I think. I walk over, kicking Henry. I'm not sold. I aim, shooting him between the eyes. "He's dead now."

"Jesus, Cole."

"Don't act like you wouldn't double-check, D. Do you want this prick popping back up?"

He groans. "Not the point. Let's find the other prick."

Conrad can be anywhere in this place, and we should've split up as soon as we stepped foot inside. But Henry got under our skin as he has always done. I take off for the bedrooms and don't care where the guys go. We need to find Conrad before he leaves the compound.

Taking the stairs two at a time, I reach his room quickly. The door was left wide open; I've been in this situation before. I know he has a gun, and most likely, this will be the shootout Dorian wanted. With a deep breath, I poke my head around the door frame. His room is bare. I was expecting something more from a vice president. All that's in here is a bed and dresser.

Living the high life, I see.

The bedroom seemed empty, so I took the chance and stepped inside. My eyes slowly adjust, taking in the room. The window is still open from where he shot at Nyx. If he was stupid enough, he could've jumped. Treading softly, I reach the window; looking outside, I can't see past the yard light.

Getting frustrated, I head to the room next door. I'll tear each room apart if I have to. He has to be here somewhere. The guys haven't called out, and I haven't heard anything, so they haven't found him either.

I storm down the stairs.

"Where are you, you fuckin' prick? Scared to face us?" I holler into the common area.

I spin around, stopping in front of the bar. Two sets of voices came from this direction when we first came in. There's a spot at the bar where the keg sits, and I bet any money he's hiding there. I silently lift myself on top of the bar, peeking over the ledge.

Dorian appears in the corner of my eye. I nod below me. Dorian moves to block the exit of the bar. I'm not sure where Nyx is, but if he needs a break, that's fine. I hold up my fist, counting to three. My third finger is barely up, and I jump off the bar, landing on the ground.

It's a risk; he could blow my kneecaps out.

A risk that never happened. "Where the fuck is he?"

"I searched everywhere, but he isn't inside." Dorian places his gun on the bar top.

This is getting frustrating. Where the hell did he go? Fuck this. I head to the main light switch, turning it on, eliminating the entire space. At this point, I don't care if anyone knows we're here. Lifting my mask, I get a better look at the place.

"Where can he go? I didn't hear an engine start."

"He could've left on foot." Dorian lifts his mask, looking toward the front door.

I shake my head. "No, he's on the property. Hiding, he knows what's coming. We need to find Nyx."

Dorian heads to the kitchen, and I go to Henry's office. We should've been gone by now; leave it to Conrad to delay us. I didn't realize how messy Henry's desk was. But I'm looking for one thing, shuffling papers to the side, tossing half-eaten sandwiches on the floor.

The desk drawer is locked, and that's how I know it's in there. I'm not searching that body for the key; giving it a good tug, the drawer pops open. Only he would leave it here, fuckin' idiot.

"Found, Nyx."

I jerked my head up. "Where?"

"He's in the garage."

I grab the set of keys for Coleman's place and follow Dorian.

The garage is lit up when we reach it. Stepping inside, Nyx is waiting for us.

He spins his mask in circles around his finger, shooting us a grin. "I found the fucker."

"Where? We searched everywhere for him." Dorian's voice went rough.

Nyx shakes his head. "You wouldn't believe it."

"Jesus, Nyx, we're wasting time." My patience is running thin, and the clock is ticking.

He points to the cellar door. "Down there. Scaredy cat won't come up."

Hmm. "I wonder why?"

"Well, I'm not sure we are friendly. He just doesn't want to play." Nyx grins.

Dorian stomps on the door. "Dick face, you still alive down there?"

Boxes fall over, and metal hits the floor. "I assume he is." Chicken shit. "Lift the door. If he doesn't come up alone, I'll drag the bastard up."

I stand to the side, aiming my gun, and Dorian does the same. Nyx reaches for the handle on the cellar door; he looks between us and nods. With a quick pull, it's open. My heart jumps when we're met with darkness. The worst part, the stairs are open.

"Be careful, Cole," D warns.

I turn around, taking the first step. Headed into the unknown, my heart is in my throat. Conrad could be watching me.

"If you jump me, I'll shoot you in the dick and leave you to die a slow and painful death."

"You'll kill me anyway, so what does it matter?" His voice echoes off the walls.

I reach the bottom step, and the hairs on my neck raise. He's somewhere near me. "Fuckin' rights, I'll kill you, but I'd rather do it when you're up there. Carrying your body isn't worth it."

My eyes take forever to adjust to the dark, taking tiny, quiet breaths. I wait until Conrad moves. Feet shuffle to my right, turning, a fist enters my view. I'm too slow at dodging, and my eyes water from the pain. *Sonofabitch.*

Conrad chuckles. "Not so tough in the dark, are ya?"

I wipe away the blood. "Oh, I'm tough. I don't have to take cheap shots."

"No, that's Nyx, isn't it."

That's a low blow. He's lucky I didn't send Nyx down here. "Face me, and we'll fight man to man."

He emerges from behind the pile of boxes, and I have to resist the urge to shoot him in the head.

"Drop the gun, Cole."

I laugh. "Drop yours first."

The clang of his gun hitting the floor is almost a relief. Somehow, I don't trust him. The thought of dropping my gun kills me. I'll kill him later. Dropping my gun, I stare at him.

"Are we gonna finish this or what?" I ask through gritted teeth.

Conrad steps forward. I need to control myself no matter how much I want to beat the shit out of him. He rushes for me; I think he forgot that I'm the club's enforcer. Grabbing his arm, I swing him around, jabbing him in the kidney. He falls to the ground, crying out in pain.

"Remember your place. You think you can win against me?" I punch him hard in the jaw, knocking him out. "Pussy." I whistle for the guys.

"What's wrong?" Nyx yells down.

"I need help to get him up the stairs."

Dorian slides down the stairs. "Jesus, I can't see shit. Where are ya?"

"You're almost on top of me."

"You did a number on him." Dorian kneels next to me.

I roll my eyes. "What I wanted to do was shoot him and leave him down here, but we would've had to haul him up either way."

I collect my gun and grab Conrad by the arms, and Dorian grabs his legs. Lift and shove; I don't care how it gets done.

"Cole," Dorian grunts. "Think of a better plan next time."

I hike Conrad's arm higher over my shoulder. "I'll keep that in mind for next time."

Coleman's death will be quicker and easier.

We move Conrad into the torture room. Now, it's a waiting game for him to wake up. Nyx rechecks the time.

"How hard did you punch him?"

I cringe. "I'm not sure. I didn't think it was that hard."

He shakes his head, leaving the room. Dorian glances at me and shrugs. I gave up asking questions about what Nyx does; I rechecked Conrad's restraints. The last thing I want is for him to get free when he does wake up.

"I'll wake him up, move." I back up in time for water to be splashed all over Conrad.

Conrad wakes with a deep inhale.

"Nice, watch out dickhead." Nyx throws the bucket at Conrad's head.

Conrad is slow at reacting and doesn't see the bucket coming. His head snaps back from the force. We all couldn't help but laugh.

"That was hilarious, man. You should've seen your face," Nyx snorts.

I head to the table we have filled with tools. I want to make this last, but I want to return to Catalina. I grab a pair of pliers. I'll cause him some pain before ending his shitty life.

"Fuck you, Cole," Conrad spits out.

I wave the pliers in his face. "Are you sure? I can fuck you with these if you want?"

Dorian holds Conrad's head back, knowing what I'm planning. Nyx digs his fingers into Conrad's jaw. Conrad fights us when I bring the pliers closer to his mouth.

"When was the last time you saw the dentist?" Conrad screams louder the closer the pliers get to his teeth. His body shakes in the chair as I clamp down on his back molar. Needing leverage, I kneel on his leg. With a tight hold, I pull. Blood pools in his mouth, but I keep going. Dead people don't need teeth. His screams die down, and the fight leaves his body.

"Think he's had enough?"

Nyx chuckles. "I always knew he was a pussy. Never could tough it out. End his miserable life."

I move away, and Dorian drops Conrad's head. Blood drips onto his shirt.

Conrad mumbles something.

"Sorry, didn't catch that?"

He lifts his head. "I said fuck you," he slurs.

Dorian sighs. "Even after ripping half your teeth out, that's your comeback?" He shakes his head. "Ever wonder why no one gave you respect in the club? No one cared about you." He walks backward until he reaches the table. "Did you want to pick the weapon, or should I?"

His eyes flashed with fear as Dorian grabbed a knife. Dorian slips his mask back on before heading in Conrad's direction again. Nyx and I follow, surrounding Conrad.

Dorian cups Conrad's neck, touching foreheads. "No hard feelings?" With a quick jerk, he sinks the knife deep under his ribcage, driving it into his heart. Conrad gasps for air.

"How are you feeling, D?"

"I'm getting tired of this night already. Two down."

We're only getting started.

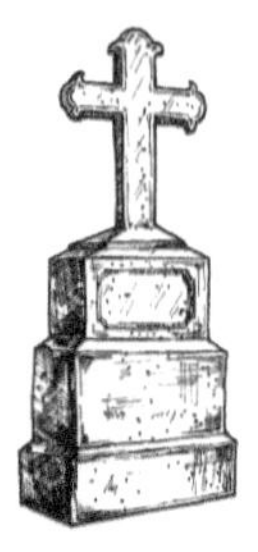

23

DORIAN

I can't wait until I'm back in bed, wrapped in the warmth of Catalina. When I signed up for tonight, I wasn't expecting it to be so hard. I can't blame Freddy; what Henry did was unexpected. That completely blindsided us. To go after an old man for what we had planned. No wonder why Nyx lost his shit.

I'm trying to resist the urge to beat him as I roll his body in the tarp. I gave this man three years of my life and got nothing in return. Fuckin' nothing. Not a lick of respect; he couldn't even call me by my first name. Always *boy*.

I hate when it's time to go with my parents. I love staying with Grandmother. And she spends time with me and doesn't yell when I do something wrong. They haven't even picked me up, and I can already sense what's coming. I don't understand why they keep trying to be my parents when they don't want me. I've known since I was five that they didn't care about me. I'm not stupid; a kid can tell when they aren't being loved.

"Dorian, sweetheart. Your parents are here." Grandmother pokes her head into my room.

My shoulders drop. "Do I really have to go? You're his mom. Tell him no."

She steps into my room, kneeling on the floor next to me. "Listen to me. This won't last forever. One day, when you're older, you can make your own decisions. The world will be your apple. But until then, you'll have to spend time with your parents."

Tears sting my eyes. "I don't understand. They don't like me. Why do they keep doing this to me?"

She cups my face. "I'm not sure, sweetheart. But you are loveable. I love you, and we can only hope one day they grow up before you do."

Who knew she was right? It only took them years to figure their shit out. That's when I realized I wouldn't let anyone, including this asshole, control my life. I dump Henry in the back of the van.

"Asshole," I mutter.

"Doing alright?" Nyx asks.

I chuckle. "I honestly don't know. Nyx. The past keeps coming up, and I swear I'm holding on by a thread."

"I know, this night is almost over, and we'll never have to do this again. One more, and then we can get our girl."

God, I can't wait. I need her so desperately right now.

"Here." Cole drops Conrad's body into the van. "We need to move out before Coleman changes his plans for the night."

The ride back into town is quiet until we hit the *Welcome to Eastwood* sign, and I'm blown away. The sign is burning. I'm at a loss for words. The further we drive, the more destruction unfolds. I've never seen so many stores destroyed and people running for their lives.

"Cole, this is unreal." Nyx weasels his way in between Cole and me.

"Thank the fuckin' mayor."

"I would hate to be caught in that. Your chances of surviving are slim to none." I keep driving, trying to weave between people.

The road to the mayor's place is dark, which doesn't sit right with me. His road is lined with light posts, but everyone is broken.

"Something is wrong," Cole finally speaks.

"Think someone else got to him first?"

Oh, let's hope. Our job will be easier. I just don't like surprises. Cole was sure Coleman would be bunkered down in his house, but maybe he fled early on. Pulling into the driveway, it's clear that someone has come through. The front door is wide open, and the windows are smashed out.

"Fuck," Cole hisses.

We jump out of the van and rush for the door. Stepping inside, we freeze. I've been killing people for years, but this, I've never seen anything this gruesome before.

"Holy shit, what the hell happened?" Nyx walks deeper into the house, stepping over a dead body.

Two bodies lay on the living room floor. There is blood splatter up the white couch to the ceiling. No sign of Coleman yet. We follow the blood trail into the kitchen, and I'm shocked Nyx hasn't barfed yet. If Coleman is in this house, he's got to be dead. The amount of blood can't be from the two bodies.

"I say we search upstairs. If he did escape, I would be shocked." Cole rubs his face, his mouth forming a grim line.

"I almost want to ask questions, but in a way, I don't. You have to be a sick bastard to do this." I understand we pulled Conrad's teeth out before stabbing him, but those bodies were stabbed more times than necessary.

Nyx groans but turns for the stairs. "I swear if he's still alive, I'm not waiting—I'm shooting on sight."

Coleman can't live like the peasants in town, his stair-case splits with the left side entering his office and the right heading down the hall to the rest of the rooms. I head for the office; I'm getting so tired of searching for people. His office is empty, minus all the blood from somebody venturing in here; I'm about to walk to his desk when Cole yells.

"Dorian."

Please say they found him. I head in the direction of Nyx and Cole's voices.

"I swear, Cole, I'm done. I can't keep doing this."

"You have no choice. We all agreed we would do this. It's not over until Coleman is dead."

I walk in, finding them arguing over Coleman's body.

"Is he dead?" I ask, walking closer.

"No, he's passed out." Nyx turns to me. Someone did us the favour and tied him to his bed for us.

I slap Coleman across the cheek, and his eyes spring open.

"W-what's going on? Release me." He pulls at his restraints.

I roll my eyes. I took my gun out, resting it between his eyes. Coleman stops moving, and his eyes grow wide. "I wanted to shoot you on sight. I'm tired of this night, and it's all thanks to you. Why couldn't you just find a fuckin' hooker and call it a night? Why invent a stupid night like this? Are you happy with how it turned out this year? Do you know your downstairs is painted red?"

"Of course I'm not happy," Coleman scoffs. "I wanted this town to be a place for others to visit and talk about. Who wouldn't want to visit a town that offered a night of fake purging?"

"Fake purging. Are you kidding me?" Cole's voice turns sour. "You know what the guys do in this town every Halloween? It gets talked about all right, but not for the reason you want. You disgust me."

Nyx closes his eyes, taking a deep inhale. "I can't imagine what went through your head to think this would be a good idea. Your wife's pussy not working, or she finding it someplace else? Is that why you wanted this? You know what? Doesn't matter anymore. You're done. Dorian, just shoot him already."

"No, please, you can't do this."

I'm over this shit. I pull the trigger ending his life and the bullshit he has over this town.

"About time. What a bunch of bullshit, not even an apology." That's what pisses me off the most. Not an ounce of regret. Whatever, it's done.

"Are we leaving the other two bodies?"

Cole steps to the window, looking out. "I'm not touching them. Whoever stumbles in here tomorrow morning can deal with that issue."

It's almost a relief to be getting to the cemetery. Our task is complete, and once they are in the ground, we can finally get back to Riley's and grab Catalina. This nightmare will be over. I'm not even sure what hour we're at.

I'm glad we chose the cemetery out of town. It's still quiet out here. Doesn't surprise me. There aren't people to fuckin' murder. Realistically, we could've brought Cat out here, and she probably would've been safe.

"We'll do this quick. I'm worried Riley's place might've been attacked." Cole stares out his window.

Nyx whispers, "I fuckin' hope not."

I hop out, heading for the back doors. Nyx greets me with a small smile. "Almost over bud."

"I know. Thank God we dug those holes already."

We each take a body and start dragging. With a big kick, the body drops into the hole. I salute the cunt and grab the shovel. I'm halfway filling the grave in when I hear leaves crunch behind me. I look over and see the guys freeze.

I go to reach for my gun. "I wouldn't do that, Dorian. Or you two."

I peek over my shoulder to see two guys standing there with LED masks on. One is yellow, and the other is orange.

"Catalina's brother, I'm guessing," Cole asks.

"Brothers, where is she?" Orange-masked dickhead says.

"Like we would fuckin' tell you, little assholes." Nyx laughs. "Are you shittin' me? What the fuck do you want, anyway?"

They laugh in return. "I don't think you have an option. Momma, have at it."

Momma? What the hell does that mean? A loud buzzing noise comes behind me, the painful bite into my neck. "Ahh, fuuck." I try to scream. My teeth clench tight, and no matter how much I fight, my body falls to the ground; when I look above me, a woman with blonde hair grins at me. My body jerks like a fish out of water.

She kneels down next to me, pulling out a pair of cuffs. "I would apologize, but there's nothing to say."

I have plenty to say, you fuckin' bitch. You wait until I can move again. You'll be in a hole, too. I look past them, noticing the white van. Motherfucker.

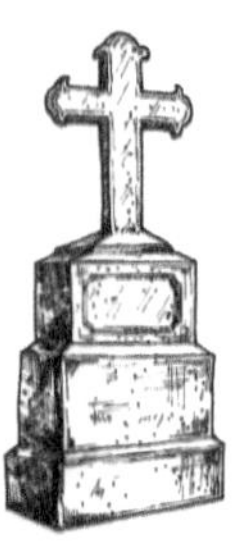

24
CATALINA

I've never been in this much pain before. Every step I take feels closer to the ground. Riley has been amazing, and how he escaped without being killed still blows me away. He still won't tell me how many people he ended up killing. I don't think he wants to think about it anymore than I want to. Which, honestly, works for me. I want to forget about this night. The school comes into view, and I'm relieved.

We've been lucky and have been able to dodge a few crowds of clowns running around. I think they had other things on their minds, thankfully. It's getting harder to tell who wants to murder and who's just out trying to ruin the town.

"Can you hold yourself up so I can unlock the door?"

I nod. "Yeah, I'm good." Resting my head on the wall, I wait. The knife is still sticking out of my shoulder, and I haven't been brave enough to pull it out yet. Riley wouldn't touch it.

Riley guides me inside, heading for the lab. "I'll try to fix you up, but I'm no doctor."

"That's fine. I'll try to be a good patient. But no promises."

He leaves to find his supplies, and I try to distract myself. My thought wanders to Dr. Deadbodies. I hope he's safe tonight. I should've sent him a text or something. It's not like I've had many people to check on.

"All right, I found little, which surprises me, considering this is the medical area. Then again, I don't have access to every space. Don't bleed out on me." He touches the knife, and I hiss. "Fuck, don't. I don't think I can do this."

"Yes, you can. Please, Riley. I need you too." Shivers rolled down my back.

He rubbed his temples. "Yeah, okay." He grabbed some gauze and some antiseptic. "Should we count down or?"

"Pull it on three." I clench my teeth and wait for him to count.

"One...Two." And he pulls.

My stomach turns, and my body falls towards the floor. Riley's hand slams hard into my shoulder, and his other stops my body from going anywhere.

"Catalina? You with me?" his voice uneasy, almost fearful.

I try to answer, but I'm so dizzy. Maybe we should've left the knife until the morning and gone to the hospital.

"Riley," I slur. "I'm not feeling so good."

"Stay awake. I can't do this alone. We made it this far, but I have to stitch it closed and—" He's quiet.

"Yeah?"

He clears his throat. "I don't have meds to freeze you."

Balls. "Do it, can't hurt any worse than the knife." I need to think of other things, but it's hard when I know what's about to happen. I need to know if the guys are doing okay. I should've asked more questions about where they were going; It's club business as far as I know.

"We need to take your sweater off."

Oh, holy hell. "Just cut it so you can work. I'm not taking it off."

"I don't have anything to cut it with." I raise a brow staring at the knife, and he cringes. Thankfully, it's not a favourite shirt, or I would be extra pissed.

"You need to hold this." He grabs my hand, making me press the gauze to my wound. He pulls the collar away and starts cutting away; he swears when my wound is fully exposed.

"How bad is it?" I try to take a glance down, but the world spins.

He ignores me and grabs the needle and thread. "I'm gonna start now." He nods like he's trying to convince himself more than anything.

I nod fast and grip the table. I will myself not to pass out and be strong for the guys. I need to find them still before my brother does. Every time Riley pokes me with the needle, I become light-headed and dizzy.

"Riley, I'm gonna pass out now."

"Shit."

My head bobs forward, and then it's black.

The throbbing in my right shoulder wakes me. I'm praying this night is over; it has to be morning. I try to sit up.

"Fuck."

"Yeah, you are down an arm, remember."

My eyes fly open, and Riley sits beside me, looking like death. "How long was I out for?"

"Not as long as you've been hoping for. Thirty minutes tops. But you're all stitched up, and I never want to do that again."

"Thanks." I sit up. Where did I put my phone? "Have you seen my phone?"

"Ah, I think you left it at my place."

The one thing I meant to grab, and I completely forgot about it. They could've been trying to call me this whole time; I'm so stupid.

"Cat, you can call them from the phone here."

I laugh at him. "You know, this is why you're going far in life, my friend."

"You're also in pain, and that brain isn't working. I'll help you off the gurney."

I call Cole first, and it rings and rings. Not wanting to be that girlfriend, I call Nyx next. When he doesn't answer, I'm starting to get worried. Come on, Dorian has to answer.

It rings twice and connects.

"Dorian? You there?"

"No, pretty girl. Dorian is a little tied up at the moment."

My heart stops. No, it didn't just stop. My soul left my fuckin' body.

"What's wrong? Not excited to hear from your big brother?"

The sound of his voice sends chills down my spine; deep down, I knew my brother would go after the guys. But in a way, I wish he would've come after me.

"Where are they?"

"What makes you think I'll tell you so quickly?" his voice shook with fury.

Every muscle tensed. What's the point of this conversation, then? If he won't tell me jack-shit, how am I supposed to read his mind if he won't help me?

"Jesus Christ, just tell me what you want then."

"You sure do act strong when you're on the phone, Catalina."

Riley places his hand on my shoulder, squeezing it. "Just tell me what you want?" I swallowed the lump that formed.

"I want what's owed to Momma."

"What?" I shoot Riley a puzzled look.

"Oh, don't act like you don't know. Meet me at the house." The line goes dead before I can answer.

"Cat? What's going on?"

I would rather stick needles in my fingertips than return to that house. "Riley, my psychotic family has kidnapped my boyfriends. I need to go get them."

His eyes shifted nervously in my direction. "You can't go back out there. Are you crazy?"

I might be losing my goddamn mind is the problem. I swore I would never step foot in that house again; there was never a reason to. I don't understand what he means by *what's owed to her*. I gave them everything last year when Dad died.

"I have to. Are you coming or staying?" I can do this alone if I need to. I'll be worried about him, don't get me wrong, but I can't stay.

He rubs his face and groans. "Cat, I can't let you go alone. You were fuckin' stabbed a few hours ago. What if you passed out again? Not happening. I'll drive. The van is parked out back still."

"Thank you, Riley."

I'm unsure what's worse—the drive through Eastwood, watching people destroy it for fun or the drive back to my hometown. I'm trying my hardest to keep the memories at bay, but they keep pressing to break free. Returning to Laketon is proving to be the worst memory of all.

"You grew up here?"

"Unfortunately." Passing my old high school almost makes me laugh. Even though I lived in my car, I survived the tough times. My family didn't beat me down.

But when that baby blue house appears, pain grips my heart. I should've come home at least once more to visit my dad. Or at least called him. I'm still wondering why he left all his money to me and how he acquired all of it in the first place. Was it from guilt? If that's the reason, then I'm glad I signed it over to her. But I signed it all over, so why are they coming after me again?

"What's the plan once we get in there?" Riley asks parking across the street.

"I'm not sure. Her sons are horrible people, Riley. You need to watch yourself in that house. They'll most likely be keeping the guys in the basement. We need to get to them."

Whatever they have planned, they can do it without the guys. This is between me and my family.

25

COLE

Never in my lifetime would I think I would be kidnapped. I find it funny if I think about it hard enough. Kidnapped in the fuckin' cemetery. It's ironic, isn't it? I can't figure out where we are. I watched in horror when Dorian went down by a stun gun. I was helpless, then Nyx went down, and I knew it was over.

Now we're stuck tied to a pole in a musty basement somewhere. I jiggle my hands once more, trying to break the handcuffs.

"Cole, fuck off already. They aren't going to break." Dorian spat out, drawing in a deep, harsh breath.

"How else are we supposed to get the hell out of here, Dorian?" My anger rose with every word. If he doesn't help, then I'll do it alone. Nyx hasn't spoken since he woke, and I'm getting worried.

Nyx turns, his cuffs clanging on the pole. That's the most we've gotten out of him this entire time.

"Nyx, please talk to us. We know this is killing you, too. We will get out of this," Dorian begs him.

We're greeted by silence.

"Nyx, he's telling the truth. The kidnappers have a plan. It's only a matter of minutes before they tell us what it is." I try to reason with him.

He ignores us.

"Hey, you assholes, come down here and talk to us like fuckin' men!" I yell. I'm tired of this bullshit. If they want us, they better start answering our questions.

The door swings open, slamming against the wall. Heavy footsteps descend the stairs.

"Will you shut the hell up? You'll wake Momma up."

Is this dude for real? His momma? He's worried about waking his mommy.

"You still live at home with your mommy. Aww, that's cute." I tease him.

The ass wearing the orange mask storms to me, punching me in the stomach. All the air escapes my lungs, and my body tries to fold in on itself, pulling tight on my shoulders.

"Sonofabitch," I cough.

"Watch what you say about Momma or I'll cut your tongue out." He spits out, anger radiating off his body.

"That's enough. You'll soon find out what I need from you three. Until then, keep your mouths shut," the Yellow masked asshole says.

For the likes of me, I can't remember her brother's names. She never refers to him by his name. I've only read it once on the lawyer's documents when she signed over the inheritance. I raise my eyes and smile at him.

"I'd watch your back if I were you."

He gave a brief laugh. "Yeah, and why's that?"

"Because your sister isn't one to be fucked with anymore."

I'm not playing around anymore, and I hope Catalina never finds out where we are. This will send her into a state of panic. Her brother doesn't need to know, but Catalina is stronger than last year. The three of us will get out of this together.

"Fuck you, Cole." He slams his fist into my ribs. "I guess you'll have to wait and see."

A sharp pain shoots up my side and my body sags.

"Cole?" Panic in Dorian's voice raises. "Get the fuck out of here, assholes. If you can't tell us what you want, then leave us alone."

Their footsteps pound up the stairs. Leaving us alone once again.

"I'm fine. It's not like I haven't been hit a few times before. I don't understand what they want. Is it a trap for Wednesday?"

Nyx groans—the first sound since we've been down here.

I jolt awake from the voices from above.

"What's going on?"

"I'm not sure. They started a little while ago. Whatever is going on, they aren't overly happy about it." Dorian tilts his head, watching the rafters.

I rest my head on my shoulder, looking at Nyx. His head is dropped down, staring at the floor. He hasn't made a peep since we figured they wanted to lure Wednesday here.

The basement door flies open.

"He can stay down there with them. I don't care." A female voice yells.

We all watch the stairs, waiting.

"Hurry the hell up, or I'll push you down the stairs."

"Keep your hands off me, and I'll be able to walk, you asshole."

"Riley?" Dorian whispers.

No. It can't be.

"I have a new roommate for you dickheads," The cunt in the Orange mask tells us.

Riley rounds the corner, and I'm at a loss for words. I'm so confused and don't understand what is happening. He must see something and shakes his head slightly. Orange mask shoves him so hard that he falls to the cement floor.

"I'll guess that'll be your home. I don't have time for your bullshit. You shouldn't be here." He tears his arms up, and a popping sound explodes in the basement. Riley's voice cracks as he screams. But dickhead ignores his cries and ties his hands to a metal rod. He shoots us a glare before storming up the stairs.

We're left in silence as Riley draws in shaky breaths. Luckily popping a shoulder into place is easy; it's getting out of the handcuffs that are proving to be a pain in the ass.

"Riley? Doing all right?" I cautiously ask.

He draws in a deep breath, lifting his head. "Not really. But I'm not bleeding, so that's a plus."

That's good. "Wanna tell us what's going on?"

"Like, why the fuck you're here," Dorian adds.

"Where the fuck is Catalina, Riley?" Nyx lashed out. Pulling hard on his cuffs, trying to get to Riley.

Fear twisted in my gut when Riley turned pale. That answers the question.

"She's upstairs," he spoke, the words barely reaching me.

Nyx loses it.

He bangs his cuffs on the pole and screams for them to let Cat go. My heart can't take anymore; a piece breaks off with every scream. The need to be with her and to hold Nyx is killing me.

"Nyx, we'll get her. I swear, even if it kills me, we will get her."

He yells once more. Then he turned to me, and his eyes darkened with pain. "Don't make promises you can't keep Cole. I'll burn this house to the ground with all of us in it if I have to."

"Riley, what do they want from her?" Dorian asks the question that I've been thinking the entire time.

He shakes his head. "They never told her. They only kept saying they wanted what was owed."

"The fuck does that mean?" Nyx spits out.

"She didn't know either. She said she paid them." He shrugs and then cries out in pain.

The inheritance money? She signed that over. What the hell is going on up there?

"Can anyone get free?" I ask even though I know the answer.

"No," they all say.

26

CATALINA

I knock on the door, and I can sense doom lurking on the other side of the door. Riley, Jesus. He should've stayed behind. I'm placing him in the worst situation of his life. The purge will resemble child's play compared to what greets us behind this door.

The door swings open, and I'm face-to-face with him. His mouth twitched into a knowing smile. One that said, I still have control over you.

"Well, if it isn't the slut. Welcome home. Momma missed you." Then his eyes look past me and harden. "Who the fuck is this?" he spits out.

"A friend."

"Get the fuck inside now." I bite my lip as he grabs my sore arm, dragging me inside the house. "Tell your friend to join us."

I stare at Riley, and thankfully he follows.

The house hasn't changed at all. The same beige paint on the walls tells me she hasn't changed her taste and thinks beige goes with everything. He keeps dragging me until we reach the living room. I'm surprised they changed the couches. It must've been with the money they collected.

I let out a laugh.

"What's so funny?"

"Oh, nothing." Riley moves next to me, and my brother's heads snap at him.

"Is this another one of your boyfriends?"

Riley goes to answer, but I give him a nudge. "Don't worry about him. What do you want?"

Then I smell her daylilies and peonies. Her scent hasn't changed, and it sends chills down my spine. I don't need to turn around to see the anger and hate on her face. I can feel it on the back of my head.

"Well, if it isn't the daughter and her? What is he?"

"No clue. They won't talk."

Fuckin' rights we won't talk. If they can't tell me where the guys are and why I'm here, then we don't speak. Highways work in both directions, assholes.

"Catalina, where's the rest of the money?" she asks pleasantly.

I want to vomit. I raise a brow, confused. "I signed over the paperwork a year ago. Perhaps you spent it?"

She struck faster than I thought she would. The crack of her hand on my cheek stings the same. "Watch your fucking mouth." Her voice rose with each word. "I know there's more money. Where is it?" she yells.

"I don't know what you're talking about," I said through clenched teeth.

"Get him in the basement with the others. If she doesn't talk, we'll make her."

Her sons grab for Riley; I yell and dodge after them. Fingernails dig into my fresh stab wound, and I fall to the floor.

"Riley, I'll get you. I promise," I grit out.

"Don't worry about me, Cat." He fights his way, but my brothers shove him to the basement door.

Mother laughs. "Don't be so foolish. You won't be saving anyone in that basement, you little whore." Her fingers dig more, drawing blood from my wound.

I'll fight for those men down there. I'm not the same girl who left this house three years ago. She knows nothing about me. I'm not being ruled by them anymore. Screams come from downstairs, and my heart lurches. What did they do?

"Guess they couldn't help themselves after all. You best remember that, Catalina. Now speak before they do the same to you."

"I don't know anything." I managed to suppress the tears swelling in my throat.

She shoves me away. "Don't lie to me."

I want to apply pressure to my shoulder, but that would satisfy her. I will myself to stand without flinching. My only other thought is where the other two youngest sons are.

"Where are Quinn and Lane?"

She scoffs and rolls her eyes. "Don't mention their names to me. They are nothing to me."

I see the ivory castle walls are falling. Or beige, I guess. "Aww, did they realize their mother is a bitch?" I've waited years to say that to her.

Her face turns a lovely shade of crimson. "How dare you speak to me like that in my house."

"What's wrong, Momma?" Both brothers come racing toward her.

She points at me. "This whore called me a bitch."

I need to channel my inner Cole. I'm stronger than before, and these assholes have my boyfriends locked up in the basement. I still need answers, though.

"What money are you guys talking about? Why are you dodging my question?"

My mother storms down the hall, leaving me alone with the devils.

"What did you do to Riley?"

They both laugh, and goosebumps rise along my skin the louder they laugh. "That guy had what was coming. He won't be a problem anymore."

Hollowness hit my stomach; this is my fault. "You'll fuckin' pay for this." I blinked the tears back. They both shrug. It was as if an electric current had gone off. I leapt through the air, going after my oldest brother, screaming as I tumbled us over.

"You douche waffle, you're lucky I don't fuckin' shoot you between the eyes," I shout in his face. I haul off and knee him in the nuts. "You won't be needing them." Then spit on his face. He yowls in pain. Before I can register anything, I'm thrown across the room, landing on the floor in front of the couch.

I turn on all fours when my brother kicks me in the ribs. Falling to my forearms, I gasp for air; he pulls me up by my hair, getting into my face.

"You miserable bitch."

"That's enough, Kyle and Royce. We have things to discuss first."

I've never been thankful for that woman in my life until now.

"Fuck this bitch. I say we just end her life. We don't need her," Kyle slowly gets off the ground, holding his wounded nuts.

"How about you show me my boyfriends, before we talk anymore," I wheeze out. "Without the masks, you cowards."

They look at her, and she nods. Of course, she will.

Kyle leads, still limping. I hope I bruised them. Royce shoves me, and I need to walk slowly. I'm trying to think of a plan here. Only one comes to mind. I glare at the witch as she holds the basement door open for us.

"Hurry up. We don't have all night."

"It won't take long. I'm sure her guys will convince her to give it to us," Kyle tells her.

I'm getting angrier by the second they don't tell me. I hate going to the basement; it's dark and stinks. Holding onto the handrail, I take my first step, there are thirteen, and I need to time this correctly, or I'm fucked. Hitting step five, I brace myself and kick Kyle as hard as I can down the stairs. He has no time to correct himself; all we can do is listen in the dark as he hits step after step. The finishing hit is to the cement.

"The fuck." Royce finally flicks the light on, and we stare at Kyle motionless at the bottom of the stairs. Impressive. After all this time, it was the stairs that got him. "Catalina," he growls.

"I didn't do it. It was dark, after all."

"You best get down these stairs before I help you." His warm breath fanned the back of my neck.

I quickly race down the stairs, stepping over Kyle and making the turn. I want to break down and cry. All three guys are cuffed to the same pole I once was long ago.

"Wednesday."

"Half pint."

"Baby."

They all greet me, but it's their voices that break the dam. I collide with Nyx first. Sobbing into his chest. "I thought I lost you." I ignore the pain shooting from my shoulder. It's about them, not me.

"Shh, baby. Fuck I wish I could wrap my arms around you." I place a kiss over his heart, feeling it pulsing.

I move to Cole, and he groans when I wrap my arms around his waist. "Did they hurt you?"

"It's fine." As he spoke, his eyes stayed fixated on mine.

"It's not. If he isn't dead, I'll kill him." They hurt him, and I'm glad I pushed my brother down the stairs.

His brows lifted in surprise. "It's hot when you talk like that, but do nothing stupid."

He tilts his head, but he's still too tall. I can only reach his chin. "I love you."

He shoots me a slight grin and a nod.

"Half pint, find the key, then come back to me."

"Dorian."

"I'm good. I need you safe, and it's not down here."

I glance over my shoulder to find Royce glaring at me. He steps closer, shaking his head. That's not a good head shake. I back away from the guys, moving deeper into the basement.

"Catalina, I think you owe me," he taunts, moving closer.

Nyx sees him first, and his eyes shoot wide. "Royce?" They know him.

"Hello, fellas. No hard feelings about the club or anything?"

"Seriously? Did you join the club in hoping to track your sister down?" Cole tries to wiggle out of his cuffs.

Royce shrugs. "I mean, it worked. We found her, didn't we?" He keeps coming my way. "But now it's her time to see Momma and explain how she killed her favourite son."

I stumble backward, crashing over a body. "Riley," I cry out.

"Cat." He gives me a faint smile, and beads of sweat run down his forehead. What did they do to him?

"I'm coming, Catalina. You have no place to run."

I'm torn. Do I stay and help Riley or try to get up the stairs? Why didn't we pack any weapons before we came? I search the floor for anything sharp; the douchebags only tied Riley. He can cut himself away.

"Run, Cat," his voice was small.

"I can't leave you."

"Do it."

A hand grips my ankle, pulling me away. Too late. I'm caught.

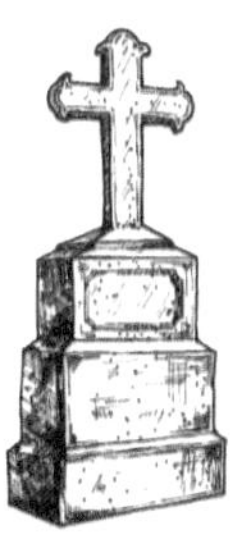

27

CATALINA

Royce drags me away from Riley. The fear in his eyes matches mine. I try to kick his kneecap with my free leg. The guys cheer me on, but it does nothing for me. My fate is sealed. I should see where it goes, but once she finds out, I killed Kyle. I don't think I'll be making it out of this house alive.

"Kyle? Royce? What's taking so long?" She calls from above.

With Royce distracted, I take my chance. I haul off and kick him hard in the knee. He drops my leg, and I scramble to get up. I only make a few feet away before my head jerks back.

"I don't think so. You can tell her what you did." He drags me backward to the stairs.

"Cat, baby, don't stop fighting. We'll find a way to get out of here." Nyx locks eyes with me.

"Remember what I told you, half pint," Dorian yells.

Royce drags me up the stairs, and I try to step on each step, but he's going too fast, and I miss them. He has a good grip on my hair, and the sting burns. I crab walk just to keep the pressure off my scalp.

Royce tosses me to the side and slams the door shut. I can hear Cole yelling through the floor. The pain rips through his voice.

"Momma."

"Where is Kyle?" She looks around like he's going to pop up.

Royce points to me. "She killed him. Pushed him down the stairs."

I stare at both of them and grin. "One down."

Royce's mouth twisted into a snarl. "You stupid whore, you'll pay for this."

"Royce, did she just say that?" She breaks into a sobbing mess. I roll my eyes; I'm over this. They don't scare me anymore.

I do, however, need to run. The basement opens to the kitchen, a slight design flaw, but it works in my favour. I race for the drawer with the knives. Pulling the drawer open, I find it empty. I run my hand deep inside, trembling when I touch nothing.

I grip the drawer, pulling it hard with a hard swing. I connect it with Royce's face. The vibration radiates up my arms. I watch as Royce staggers back, falling into the fridge. I'm positive his neck snapped. Fingers dig into my forearm, twisting my body to face her.

"I knew I should've killed you when you were a child. I never wanted a daughter. They only bring trouble, and look what you are doing to my family," she said, her tone full of steel.

"Me? You are the problem. You couldn't even tell me why you kidnapped my boyfriends. You kept giving me the runaround. What do you expect me to do?" I bit off each word, spitting them back at her.

She screams in frustration, letting go of my arm. "I got a letter in the mail a few months ago saying the lawyer had a mix-up, and you never signed all the money over."

"What money?" I snap. I move toward the living room.

"Don't act like you don't know, Catalina. Your father loved you more than he did me. Sign it over, and I'll release those boys of yours."

I shake my head. Not happening. I need her gone, too. Wait. Maybe I can twist this around.

"Fine, show me the paperwork." She shoots me a satisfying grin like she won the lottery. Maybe she has. I couldn't tell, ya.

I follow her to the office, Dad's office. Her son's pictures are still hanging in the hallway. And not one of me. It doesn't surprise me. I don't even think she took a single one of me when I was growing up. Stepping into his office brings back memories, and that's all. She changed everything in here.

She walks around the desk, grabs the folder, and passes it to me. She drops them in front of me when I don't take them.

"Here, read these and sign them. I want you gone. You ruined everything."

"Before I sign these, release the guys." I don't even look at the papers. She has two options, the way I look at it.

"Why, you little bitch."

She shoves me hard in my shoulder, throwing me off balance. Falling to the floor, I see the devil in her eyes. It's then I know who killed my father. He was trapped in this hell like I was.

"You killed him for the money? How did you know about it?"

Her mouth twitched. "Don't be so foolish. I knew for a long time he was hoarding his cash." She steps closer. "There was no way I would live the rest of my life like the middle class." She lets out an uncontrollable laugh. Bending down, she gets into my face. "I would never lower myself like some people."

Her hand moves to the back of her pants, pulling out a gun, and every nerve in my body froze. There is no way this is how I'm going out, especially if I made it this far. Fuck her. I will my body to listen to me. I need to fight to save the guys; they need me.

I'm needed.

I let out a scream and reach for her wrist; she's so shocked she staggers back, I get up and wrestle her for the gun. Her claws dig into my wrist, and it goes numb. My right arm is growing weak, and I force myself to use every cell of strength. Clenching my hand, I haul off, punching her in the stomach. She tears her fingers from my skin, leaving red marks behind. The gun tumbles to the floor, and my heart lurches.

"You'll pay for everything, Catalina," she hisses, smacking me on the cheek.

My eye waters from the smack; I should've seen it coming. She always went for the face.

"You hit like a girl." I drop to the floor, grabbing the gun. Lying on my back, I pull the trigger.

It's quiet. I stare at her, blood running down her pink blouse from where I shot her in the heart. She makes a slight gurgle sound, tumbling to the floor.

I move closer. "Where are the keys?"

"Catalina," she coughs, blood splatters on her chin.

"Answer the question." I point the gun at her head. "Please, tell me."

Her eyes slowly fall shut. I kneel, giving her a shake. "Tell me where the keys are."

"Fuck!" I drop her like a bag of potatoes. "Fuck you. Couldn't give me one thing before you left."

I have to hold back the kick I want to land on her. Let the dead rest. Right. Those rules don't apply to me. With a grin, I spit on her. "Have fun in hell." I turn to leave when I remember those stupid papers. I'm kind of curious; swiping them off the desk, I rush for the guys.

I'm halfway down the stairs when hushed voices greet me. All I want to do is cry because I'm not sure how I'll be able to free them. Stepping over Kyle's body, Nyx sees me first.

"Baby? What's wrong?"

"I can't free you." I pressed my fingers to my lips, holding back a cry.

"Yes, you can. All you need is something that can cut the cuffs. No one said you need the keys," Cole's deep calms me.

I take a deep, calming breath and turn to Riley. I owe this to him.

"Riley?" I race to his side, taking him in. "Riley? I'm so sorry."

"It's not your fault, Cat. Stop it," his voice cracks.

I check his wrists out and think I can get him untied. I look back at the guys, and Dorian nods. I nod back and go ahead and start untying him.

"This is gonna hurt, Rye Rye." I free his wrists, and his arms drop. He lets out a blood-curdling scream. "Fuck, I'm sorry. What do I do?"

The guys tell me what to do, and I get Riley into position. I hope he forgives me after this. I grab his arm, place my foot on his side, and pull. His grunts make me want to stop, but I keep going. The slip of his shoulder into place is a relief, not only to me but to Riley.

"Thank fuck," he groans.

My body is slowing down, but I can't let the guys see it. I bypass them and go up the stairs again. I have a feeling those keys are in her pocket. She wouldn't trust Royce or Kyle with them. I take the stairs two at a time, rushing down the hall. I stop in the office doorway, trying to catch my breath.

"Please have the keys." I slowly walk to her side, swallowing the lump. I bend down, reaching for her pant pocket. You would think with all the dead people I touch, I would be used to this. But I want to vomit. Deep down, I'm waiting for her eyes to pop open and her hand to reach out and grab me.

"Hurry the fuck up, Catalina," I tell myself. My blood spikes when my fingers dip into the pocket.

Nothing.

I reach over her body, digging into her other pocket. The clink of keys gives me a jolt.

"Thank you, Lucy."

I run back toward the basement, slowing down on the stairs, or I'll be like Kyle.

"I have the keys," I yell, racing to Nyx first.

"Good job, baby. I can't feel my arms anymore."

I reach on my tiptoes, getting the key in. I work fast, trying to get him free. When his arms wrap around my waist, I feel a part of my soul reconnecting. Giving him the key, I backed away. My body officially finished for the night.

I sink against the pile of boxes, trying my hardest to stay awake. I look down at my shoulder, noticing fresh blood. *Oh shit.*

"Catalina," Cole said, dropping to my side. "Wednesday, what's wrong?" He gently lifts me into his lap. "She's bleeding," he yells.

"What do you need?"

"We need to leave."

I curl deeper into Cole's chest, blocking everyone out. I wanna go home.

28
NYX

We survived the night. That's all that matters. I can't believe she placed her life at risk for us. I would've been okay with dying in that basement. I was at peace hanging there until I died. Watching Cole carry her up the stairs breaks me. She never once complained that she was in pain; her only worry was getting us out.

I help Riley up, bracing his arm. This guy has gone through hell, too. He has proven himself to be a loyal friend to Cat. I don't wanna say my chat with him had anything to do with it, but I'm just sayin' it had something to do with it.

The thought that she had to kill her family also doesn't sit right with me. That should've been something that we had to do. Those images will haunt her for life. She needs support right now, and I'll gladly give it to her once we get home.

"I parked the van outside. The keys are in my pocket," Riley tells me when we reach the top step.

"Back pocket?"

"Who places keys in their back pocket?" he shot back, raising his brows.

"I swear if I touch your dick." I reach into his front pocket, staying away from his inner thigh. "Riley, perhaps it's the other pocket."

"Bud, you're the one that dove into that pocket."

I take a deep breath, trying not to punch him. "Cole, take Cat outside." I need her out of this house fast and Dorian to burn it down. The fewer memories for her, the better. I dig into Riley's pocket quickly, and he chuckles.

"That's my dick," he whispers.

"Ah, fuck no." I pull out fast with the keys. "You're a dick."

He flinches when he shrugs. I can't think about his dick; I need to think about getting out of this town and getting everyone home. I push him to the front door, following the guys out.

Entering Eastwood, I'm in shock. It's way worse than we left it, and it makes me feel a little better knowing that Coleman is dead. I would be more excited about it if Cat would wake up. She passed out in Cole's arms and hasn't woken since.

The streets of Eastwood remind me of a zombie apocalypse. The fires left the coffee shop, where we usually met Freddy every Sunday a charred mess. Devastation all over town, and I can't look anymore. Trying to get to the hospital takes longer than expected. The cops are all over town detouring traffic; I'm surprised they wanted anything to do with us after yesterday.

"It's going to take forever to see a doctor," Cole complains about the tenth time since we showed up. The waiting area is filled with people sporting every injury.

"There's nothing we can do about it; she's breathing, and that's all that matters. She worked herself hard and is exhausted, Cole. She'll be fine," Dorian tells him before walking away.

The only lucky one was Riley; a nurse was able to sling him up, and then he went home. Cole was insistent on getting Cat checked over by a real doctor. Her shoulder stopped bleeding, but he's overreacting. She's alive and well. If I don't tell myself that I'll explode.

"Catalina Wilson," a nurse calls.

We all stand, walking with Cole. The nurse blushes as she studies us. Sorry, sweet cheeks, my heart is taken. She raises her hand, stopping us.

"Only family allowed."

Dorian broadens his shoulders, stepping close to the nurse. "She's my reason to breathe every morning, my motivation to never give up, so don't tell me only fuckin' family."

Her eyes widen in shock. "I'm sorry, but rules are rules, sir."

Oh, shit. I move fast, placing my hand on Dorian's shoulder. "Hey, big guy, we're making a scene, and Cat needs to get back there. We'll wait out here. Cole will be with her the entire time. Yeah?"

He shrugs me off. "Yeah, whatever." He storms off to the exit.

"Cole, please."

"I will, don't worry, stay with D."

I bury my lips into Cat's hair. "Wake up soon for me, baby." I squeeze Cole's arm, turning to chase after Dorian.

I find him outside, sitting on the bench. I feel his pain; we're all worried and pissed. It's natural I also get that, but fuck, I want to be with her.

"Nyx, I don't wanna talk." He speaks before I sit.

That works for me.

I'm not sure how long we've been out here, but my ass has gone numb. When I look over, my world stops. Her eyes gleamed with tears as a smile spread across her face. Cole cradles her arm, helping her across the parking lot. Her face isn't as pale, and relief floods through me.

"Catalina, baby." I took off toward her. Wrapping my arms around her waist, I bury my face in her neck, breathing her in. "Fuck, baby. You had me scared to death."

She wraps her arm around me. "I'll never leave you, love. I swear." I pull away, and her violet eyes blaze into mine. I stroke her cheek, feeling her body tremble.

"I love you, Catalina. But I swear to God, if you pull this shit again, I'll pull you over my knee and spank you." I threaten her.

Her lips fall apart. Running my thumb over her bottom lip, I tilt her head back. "Now kiss me." She blinks and licks her lip and the tip of my thumb. I lower closer, gently wrapping my hand around her neck, pressing our lips together. "I meant what I said." I kiss her once more, sensing Dorian behind me.

"Darling. Don't do that to me again, please."

Of course, he makes his quick and sweet.

It's been a week since shit hit the fan, and Cat has been home. She's been healing slow and steady, and I can tell it's killing Cole. He wants her back to normal so he can return to his normal routine, which we don't have.

The town is still being cleaned up. The body count is over fifty and rising. More bodies are being found as more rescuers dig through the rubble. They found Coleman's place empty; he's presumed to be missing.

Missing in a hole, more like it. I'm sure they'll find him. Eventually.

Cat was determined to return to school and wanted to finish her work and graduate next month. I want to be positive and think that'll happen, but honestly, I don't think it will. Her shoulder has limited mobility, and her art pieces demand lots of work. We try to head in after classes and help her, but we aren't very good at it. I think we cause more of a headache than anything.

The worst part is that she's been off work this entire time and is going stir-crazy. Davis told her that with all the bodies that came from purge night, she isn't needed at the medical department.

"Catalina?" I open her bedroom door finding her laying on the bed. "Can I see you downstairs?"

A smile tugged at her lips. "You're seeing me now."

"I know, but downstairs would be better."

"All right, give me ten."

I give her a thumbs up and race downstairs. The guys are in the den setting up.

"She's coming down. Are we ready?"

Dorian lights the last candle that lines the mantel, and Cole dims the light. The room is all set for her, and I hope she enjoys herself.

When she walks in, she's speechless. This was our way of saying thank you for saving our assholes. She never should've done that, but we'll forever be in her debt.

"You guys." Her hand shook as she reached for me. "Thank you, love."

I gently gather her into my arms. "You never have to thank me." I shift her to Dorian.

"Thank you, sweetheart." He bundles her in his arms.

"Thank you, darling."

She stares at Cole, and tears fall. "Dickhead," she whispers.

"Wednesday, come here." He spreads his arms wide. He drew her in, closing his arms tight. I never would have thought Cole would become the softy. He pulls her back, wiping her tears away. "No more tears." He presses his lips to hers.

I move behind her, lightly skimming my hand under her shirt. "Baby," I breathed into her ear. Sliding my hands upwards slowly, so slowly, her body presses into mine. "Be patient." Her back arches, pressing into Cole, and he groans. Kissing along her neck, I torment her before cupping her breasts. She moans as Cole kisses her again, and I pinch her hardened nipples.

"Let's get your clothes off. Dorian is waiting for you." Cole steps back, reaching his hand over his head, he pulls his shirt off. Cat licks her lips and blinks slowly. She grabs her shirt and pulls her arm out, and I help her with her sore shoulder.

"If it hurts too much, we'll stop."

"I'll be fine, and I trust you guys." She grabs my shirt and pulls it up. I bend the rest of the way so she can pull it off. She flicks my nipple piercing, and my dick twitches.

"Get on the floor and start sucking Dorian's cock," Cole demands.

She drops to her knees, and Dorian steps before her, stroking his dick.

"Relax your throat, let me all the way in." He brushes the tip along her lips before she opens, taking him in. "Ah, fuck." Holding her head, he thrusts, making her gag.

I can't take it much longer; kicking my jeans off, I fist my dick with every thrust Dorian makes. I watch Cole move to his knees, smacking Cat on the thighs as she lifts up. Fucker gets the first taste.

"Ride my face, little one." He moves between her thighs, and she sits like the good girl she is.

Her muffled moans only make Dorian breathe heavier. Fuck, it never gets old seeing her like this. Her fingers dig into Dorian's thighs as Cole grips her tighter. Her head falls back, and a silent cry falls from her lips.

Cole rolls her over, kissing her lips. "You taste like fuckin' candy." With a groan, he slips inside.

"Cole, please," she begs.

"I got you, little one." Lifting her legs to his chest, he drives in hard.

The sight of her is beautiful. I'm unsure where our future will go, but I hope it'll be forever. The three of us will never let her out of our sight again. I can promise her that even if that involves moving towns.

"I need you to come." Cole's voice interrupts my thoughts. I watch her toes curl, and he pulls her into his hips. "Good fuckin' girl, come all over my cock." Cole groans, leaning forward and kissing her. He slowly pulls out, and his cum drips out.

Dorian lays down, stroking himself. "Finish sucking me off." Dorian meets my eyes, and I know what he wants. Cat crawls over him, getting in between his leg, and I shift behind her moving her ass in the air.

"I'm gonna fuck you from behind and drive your throat down on D's dick, don't come up for air until you swallow all his cum."

"Okay."

I kneel behind her, gliding my hand over her ass, smacking it. Walking my hand along her spine, I sink into her hair, pulling her head back. "Open your mouth." She opens wide, and I look back at Dorian and slowly lower her head, making her take him all. Dorian's mouth pops open, and his eyes roll back.

I grab my dick, smacking it against her clit. The need to fill her roars inside of me. Slamming into her, my head spins from the sensation of her muscles clenching around my dick. *Fuck.* Our bodies shift forward, and all three of us moan. Dorian digs his hands into her hair, pulling her down more on his dick. I drive her hips into mine.

"Shit, she's taking it so well," Dorian hisses, flexing his hips, getting even deeper. She gags as I push her forward.

"So... Fuckin'... Well." I drive into her, needing her to come. I brush my finger over her clit, causing her walls to clench. I groan at the tightness. As I lung into her again, she explodes. I drive in harder, prolonging her climax.

"I'm coming. Get ready." Dorian groans.

Thank God, 'cause I can't hold on much longer, her hand weaves between our legs, squeezing my balls, and I see stars. I dig my fingers into her hips, thrusting long strides as I come.

"Fuck, baby. That was intense." I rest my head on her back, breathing hard.

We're all a puddle of bodies on the makeshift bed we created, and I couldn't think of any other place I'd rather be.

ABOUT THE AUTHOR

Hello, loves! I'm a Canadian romance writer who's all about the steamy and dark stuff. Horror books, movies, and music? Yes, please! I have a little true crime obsession, but I'll just call it research and pretend it's normal.
If you crave love stories that push the limits of lust, trust, and desire, you've come to the right place.

Follow me for exclusive sneak peeks, giveaways, and behind-the-scenes glimpses into my writing process. And if you want to keep up with my latest releases or connect on social media.

Let's dive into the shadows together, darlings.

ALSO BY

A HITMAN'S DUET
MYLES

CARTER

RUSSO MAFIA SERIES
UNBROKEN

UNBEARABLE

UNDENIABLE

STRANGERS OF EASTWOOD
STRANGERS OF THE NIGHT

STRANGERS OF THE TOWN

RAVENWOOD ACADEMY
ATTICUS

STANDALONE
CHRISTMAS UNWRAPPED